I0594394

GOLD DUST AND THE BILLIONAIRE

BILLIONAIRE LONELY HEARTS CLUB BOOK THREE

EDITH MACKENZIE

Gold Dust and The Billionaire (Billionaire Lonely Hearts Club Book #3):

Images © DepositPhotos – gstockstudio & pirita

Cover Design © Designed with Grace

❀ Created with Vellum

For every little girl and boy that had big dreams

CHAPTER 1

*F*reddy kept his gaze steady on the cards in front of him. Inside he felt like his innards were vibrating. The men who sat around the table all had the veneer of social, genial gentleman, but he knew they were ruthless. The big man in the corner of the room had a memorandum book with names and numbers and he always got what was owed, one way or another.

But not tonight. Tonight, the gods smiled down on Freddy, and he'd come up trumps. "Silvio, are you going to meet or fold?" Freddy tried to keep his voice coolly casual.

A bead of sweat broke out on Silvio's forehead. With his baldness and pale fleshiness, it was hard not be put in mind of a nervous boiled egg. Freddy rather liked eating them for breakfast. He knew his friends would be surprised to hear the ruthlessness of his thoughts. After all, they were quite often of the mind to think of him as lackadaisical and without ambition. Fact was, he had plenty, just no clue what to do with it.

"Silvio? What is the saying? Poop or get off the pot."

Silvio spun the thick gold ring on his index finger with

his thumb. "I've got nothing left to meet with except..." He ran a hand over his head. "I have a horse. I bought it for my wife."

"I didn't know your wife rides." Freddy had seen pictures of the woman in the society pages, and he felt a sudden pity for the beast having to lug her gargantuan frame about.

"She doesn't. There's a girl who rides him. Sally just goes to the events as his owner and gets to keep the prizes."

"Seems ... sporting."

"The horse is fully imported, bloodlines in the purple, and a stallion. Worth a bomb, and from what my wife tells me, wins everything it enters. I'm adding the horse to the wager."

Freddy quirked a brow at him, running his nail over the edge of his cards. "You're offering me a racehorse?"

"Not a racehorse. A warmblood. One that does dressage."

"A horse is a horse, I guess, old chap. Fine, I accept. Throw it in the pot." A trill of anticipation made his senses sharpen. "Now, show your hand."

Mutely, and with a gleam of triumph, Silvio revealed his straight flush.

"I do like a flush myself," Freddy murmured as he turned his cards. "Personally, I find a royal flush much more satisfying." Silvio gaped at him, revealing yellowing teeth. "Now, what's my new horse called?"

∼

"Bella, you'll never guess what I just won. And before you say anything, yes, I know it's bad that I'm gambling, but a chap needs to have a few vices. It keeps life interesting. It's a horse! Can you believe it, Bella? Remember how much fun we used to have going to pony club when we were children? Well, you loved it. I wasn't such a fan of the jodhpurs that mother insisted I wear. Old Poppy and Billy, those were our ponies names, do you remember? I don't even remember what this horse is called. I guess I'll find out. When you get this message, call me back, Bella. I know you're mad at me, but I'm just trying to be a good big brother. I miss—" The beep cut off the last of Freddy's message.

The stone he carried around in his belly grew heavier, the ice around it frigid. He flicked through his phone, his friends' names scrolling by. Landon would be in bed with his pregnant wife, Chora. Freddy kept scrolling. Alistair would be out of range until he got back to the station homestead. More names flicked by. Stirling sparked hope through him. His pal Stirling, Hollywood producer and fellow billionaire, would surely be around. He quickly pressed on his name and waited, tapping his foot while it rang. "You've reached Stirling Saint-Claire. Please leave a message." Freddy's mouth puckered. He was probably doting on his fiancée, Cassie.

Deciding there was nothing else to do, he tapped his driver on the shoulder. "Take me to Park Lane, old chap. There's a game there that has my name on it."

THE BAY STALLION lowered his head, letting out a great snort as if releasing all the tension from his body. "Good boy, Denny." Harper dropped her reins and patted the horse on both sides of his neck. "Very good boy."

Around them, the stable yard was a hive of activity, the sand arena with its white fencing having been built with the stable blocks wrapping around it. Some days, Harper liked to imagine that the younger horses were learning as their heads peered out, watching the older more experienced horses like Denny. She tangled his mane around her fingers as she headed for the gate at C. Denny was her heart horse. From the moment he'd entered her life five years ago as a horse with all the right breeding and talent and a horrendous reputation, she'd known that he was the one for her.

She still marveled that somehow, when she'd been a fresh-faced twenty-two-year-old, she'd been given the opportunity to ride him. Maybe it was because she was the only one stupid enough to take him on after he'd been kicked out of every training stable in Europe. But she'd known what she had, and she'd worked hard for it. Back when her stables only had two clients' horses and she was forced to train anything that came her way, she'd always had a burning ambition that she was going to make it. That and a good plan and strong work ethic to back it up.

Sitting deep in the saddle, she pulled Denny to a halt and slipped her feet from her stirrups before gracefully swinging her leg over to dismount. The stallion immediately swung his head around, rubbing the itchy spot he always got just above his eye on her. "Denny, this is why I can't wear white."

"You always wear white." Carol, her head groom, laughed, running the stirrups up on the saddle before undoing the girth.

"Whoever decided to make white competition wear needs to be shot. I spend more time soaking clothes than someone my age ought to." Harper undid her horse's noseband and throatlash before slipping it gently from his head and replacing it with a headcollar. "I'm too young for the in-depth laundry knowledge I have."

"You and me both." Carol grinned, taking the bridle from her and heading to the tack room.

Harper reached into the grooming box at her feet and retrieved a cookie. His soft nose gently tickling her palm, Denny took the treat from her. "Thanks for today. You tried so hard for me." The bay stallion munched slowly before nudging her again as if to say that surely he deserved another one if he'd been such a good boy. "Okay, but only one more."

Having made her way back, Carol waited while Harper gave Denny a final pat. "When you're ready, I'm going to take this great lump and give him a hose down."

Denny swished his tail, clearly unimpressed with being called a lump, but followed the groom meekly as she led him away. Harper unclipped her helmet, running fingers over damp hair. She always tried to save Denny as the last horse of the day to ride, that thing that, no matter how pear-shaped everything else might go, was sure to brighten it for her. The gravel crunched under her boots as she walked over to the bench, dragging the boot jack closer as she sat down. It was a relief when she pulled her feet free from her top boots.

She peered closer at her red socks, noticing the hole beginning near her big toe. A few quick stitches and it would last her ages longer yet. Harper sighed contently in the gentle ray of afternoon sunlight. Her sock was an awful lot like her stables. Everything was well-maintained, if a little weary. The stables were old but freshly painted with brightly-colored flowers in little baskets hanging from the eaves of the roof. Even an old wheelbarrow having lost its wheel now housed a multitude of brightly-colored petunias. The arena might not have the most fashionable, technically advanced surface, but it was well-harrowed and did the job just fine.

Harper wiggled her toes before tugging on her Wellingtons. The most important thing about her yard—her horses —were gleaming and the picture of health. With every aspect of their care scrutinized over, they definitely knew they were the lords of their domain. Speaking of which, Carol had finished scraping the water from Denny and was on her way back with him. Pushing herself to her feet, Harper headed over to start filling haynets, and then it would be time to skip out the manure from the stables again. Maybe after that she could have a nice biscuit and a cup of tea. *Maybe.*

CHAPTER 2

*H*ow *was it possible for sheets costing several thousand pounds to feel like sandpaper?* Freddy winced as light from the tiny sliver between the curtains stabbed into his brain like hundreds of tiny little forks. With infinite care, he slowly rolled onto his back, clutching at the sheets when the room began to revolve around him again and his brain felt like jelly on the plate that hadn't quite rotated at the same rate as the rest of his head.

Freddy forced his protesting eyes open. *What time is it? Scratch that, what day is it?* He stared up at the chandelier above him, each crystal perfection that, when hit by the sunlight, glimmered as if glowing from within. He was eternally grateful the light wasn't on to splinter his mind. He tried to force himself to remember details from the last few days. He'd called Bella, but then it was rare indeed for his sister to actually return his calls. He wasn't even sure if she was jolly well getting them. Freddy wouldn't put it past her boyfriend to be screening her calls.

Maybe she'd returned his call while he'd been sleeping. Fumbling for his phone, Freddy managed to knock over a blackbird sculpture. Frowning, he leaned over the side of the bed to find it peering back up at him with one opaque eye. Squinting against the stare of the judgmental avian artwork, he tried to remember if he actually owned the piece. At the very least, he was fairly certain it shouldn't be on his bedside table. Giving up on trying to solve that particular riddle, he gave one last reach to retrieve his phone. Now that he'd cleared most of the bedside table, this time he was successful.

Touching the screen, he saw a missed call from Stirling and an email notification. Emails were not a regular occurrence in Freddy's life. Once a month his banker would send reports, or his butler might pass on something that needed his attention, but as a whole there were never any surprises.

Curious, he focused his befuddled mind and opened it.

Harper Ferguson

123 Catchers Way

My wife was very upset when I broke the news to her.

Silvio

Still none the wiser, he opened the attachment and found registration papers for one Denisto II, apparently a bay stallion. Freddy flopped onto his back again. *I won a horse last night! Or maybe it was the night before.* The gardeners will have a fit when it starts trampling the roses. He closed his eyes against the throbbing pain in his temples. *Maybe it can wait a while. At least until after I've finished dying.*

THE LEGGY CHESTNUT gelding spooked at the mounting block just outside the arena again. "Really, Chester? It's the tenth time we've gone past it today and that doesn't include the times we went past it yesterday and the day before and the day before that. It's not new," Harper admonished the young horse.

She turned him off the long side of the arena and headed across the centerline, asking him to bend around her inside leg before they rejoined the arena rail again. There was a certain skill to getting gangly three-year-olds that still didn't know what all four feet were doing at the same time and turning them into polished, educated horses at the end of their time with her. Feeling Chester tense up again, she drove him forward with her seat into the contact until he softened, then she released the reins in reward. Bringing him back to a walk, she slipped the reins until she was holding them at the buckle. It was enough for the young horse today, and Harper always tried to finish each and every schooling session on a good note. Routine was the oil to her hard work.

Harper had just handed Chester over when she spied the dark Bentley pull up. She wasn't expecting any clients today, and regardless, none of them had a car that stupendously expensive. Brows furrowed, she continued to look. "Carol, are you able to deal with whoever is in that car?"

The groom turned and peered over her shoulder. "Maybe they're lost?"

"If they are, they don't seem to be in a hurry to leave." Just then a Range Rover pulled up beside the sleek car—one she recognized. Denny's owner, Silvio, stepped out and walked over to the other car, talking to the driver through the window. Odd, but at least it appeared that they were a friend of one of her owners. A man stepped out, and judging from his attire, he was not someone who spent a lot of time around stables. As they came closer, she got the nagging suspicion she'd met him before.

"Harper, it's a lovely day for a ride," Silvio greeted her, not quite meeting her eye.

"It doesn't matter if it is or not, I still ride," Harper returned levelly. She was definitely picking up on a strange vibe. She wondered where his wife was since that was who she normally had most of her dealings with.

"True, true," Silvio agreed quickly, flicking a glance to the man beside him. Where had she seen him before? "It transpires that my situation has changed, and Freddy here is the new owner of Denny. Freddy, this is Harper Ferguson, Denny's rider. Harper, this is Lord Frederick Orstwell."

The solid concrete under Harper's feet dropped away alarmingly. Denny had a new owner, and there were no guarantees that she would still be his rider. More disturbing was the fact that she now knew the man's name and it was one that she was familiar with.

"Hello, Harper. It's jolly good to make your acquaintance," Freddy greeted her urbanely.

Harper swallowed down a number of decidedly unpleasant responses that sprung to her lips. "We've met before."

"We have? Was it at the club?" It was impossible to tell if he recognized her and was playing dumb or really was, in fact, just plain dumb. Harper had her own private opinion on it.

"It was at a club, but not the sort I think you're referring to."

"I'm not sure I follow." *Of course he didn't. Why would he?*

"We met at Pony Club Camp when we were younger."

Freddy pulled his sunglasses further down his nose and peered at her closely. "Harper? Carpy Harpy? Is that you? You certainly grew up, didn't you? It's been ages. How have you been?"

Harper could feel the anger rising from deep inside her like vapor that threatened to suffocate her. "How have I been? Let me think. Certainly a lot better since the last time I saw you, considering you threw me into a pile of straw and hid my tack just before the pony club commissioner did a gear check and it stopped me from getting my certificate for horsemanship that I'd worked all summer for."

Silvio made a show of looking down at his watch. "Is that the time? Well, I'll leave you two to get reacquainted. Such a small world, you knowing each other. Good luck with the horse." Harper wasn't entirely sure who that last comment was directed to. The man fled before he could be drawn into the brewing confrontation.

Freddy didn't seem the least bit perturbed by her animosity. "I was just telling Bella the other day how much fun we had at pony club. You remember Bella, my sister, don't you?"

"Yes. I always felt sorry for her, having a brother like you."

Was that hurt she saw? "Bella might agree with you these days."

There was a loss behind those words that had Harper wondering what had happened between the siblings. Back when they'd been younger, the two had been thicker than thieves. Suddenly, inspiration hit. "Sell Denny."

Freddy stared blankly at her. "Who's Denny?"

What idiot didn't know the name of the horse he'd just paid a fortune for? At least she assumed that's what he'd paid given the stallion's value. "The horse you just bought."

He smiled sheepishly at her. "Is that his name? It doesn't sound very majestic."

"It's his stable name," she ground out.

"That's right, it was something fancier on his papers." He looked at the stables around him for the first time. "So, you want me to sell him so you can buy him?"

He made it all sound so simple. "I would give my right arm to own him. But I'm not from a rich family like you, so I can't afford him."

He looked at her like the idea of not being able to afford anything was completely foreign to him. "Why do you want me to sell him then?"

He really was an imbecile. Why did he think she wanted him to sell Denny? "Because anyone else owning Denny is preferable to you."

He gave her an infuriating smirk that sent her blood boiling. "I might just keep the horse a little longer. Who knows, I might enjoy owning a showjumper. I assume you want to continue riding him?"

"Dressage horse," she said through clenched teeth. "And yes."

"Even if I am the owner?" he baited.

Harper clenched her fists at her sides. Sighing, she released all her frustration. She knew she'd been beat. "For that horse? Even if you're the owner."

"Jolly good. Now, if there isn't anything else that needs to be discussed, I'm off."

She wanted to scream at him that there bloody well was more to discuss, that in the blink of an eye he'd upset all of her carefully laid plans for her competition career, that the thought of having to deal with him for God knows how long was enough to give her a migraine.

"No, there's nothing to discuss."

CHAPTER 3

The horse lifted its back, each movement of his legs in the passage like coiled springs. Harper held the impulsion, keeping the cadence a moment longer before allowing Denny to move forward into a working trot, releasing the pressure on the great stallion. Changing the rein across the diagonal, she prepared to collect him again, riding each movement as if she was part of the horse. It had taken her years to gain the muscle memory to be able to accomplish what she now made look so easy. When she rode, there was nothing but her and the horse.

Mirroring the exercise that she'd just completed on the other rein, this time when Denny finished the passage, she did a downward transition to walk and let him go large around the arena on a loose rein.

"I can't believe how well he did today," Carol called from the side of the arena. "Those flying changes are getting better all the time."

Harper patted Denny's glistening mahogany neck. "He was a little late behind in the first few, but he really tried. He's really stepping up a level every time I ride him."

The groom opened the gate, her enthusiasm beaming from her smile. "What competitions are we entered in next?"

Harper scrunched up her face as Denny's hooves clip-clopped on the way to the crossties. "The other horses are still on track for what we planned at the beginning of the season. After the next couple of events, I don't know for Denny. I'll have to ask his new owner." Gosh, it frustrated her to admit that. Why on earth did that new owner have to be Frederick Orstwell?

She bounced lightly on the balls of her feet as she dismounted. Harper Ferguson hadn't made it this far by being a quitter. She was just going to have to find a way to deal with him or, if she was lucky and what was more likely the case, he'd lose interest and sell the horse. Her stomach twisted in knots at the thought that, with that new owner, there was no guarantee that Denny would remain with her. Harper ran up the stirrups on her saddle as Carol unbridled the bay stallion. *Maybe it was a case of better the devil you know.* If she was lucky, he'd forget that he even had a horse, and as long as his banker kept paying the bills, she could be left in peace to get on and get the job done. Feeling happier than she'd felt for days, she turned to her groom.

"I'll hose him down if you want to start mixing feeds."

Untying him, Harper began to make her way to the wash bay, fantasizing about the solarium her old coach had set up at his establishment, not to mention the aqua walker. "One day, boy," she whispered to Denny as she secured him, rubbing him gently in his favorite spot at the base of his ear. "One day."

FREDDY PULLED BACK the edge of his cuff, exposing the platinum Rolex at his wrist. He was beginning to wonder if Bella had stood him up. When she'd called him yesterday unexpectedly, he'd been in a state that hovered between anger, shock, and hope. It was just the sort of tsunami of emotions that proper British gentleman avoided like the plague.

"Quit looking at your watch, I've arrived," Bella declared dramatically. Freddy grinned at his sister as he stood to give her a kiss on the cheek, and then held her chair out for her. She was perfectly groomed as always, managing to look both glamourous and classy at the same time.

"Hello, sister dear, I was starting to think you were quite simply a figment of my imagination."

"You haven't the talent to imagine someone as fabulous as me for your sister." She gracefully lowered herself into the seat, pulling her oversized sunglasses from her face as she peered up at him mischievously. "I am quite simply incomparable."

"An incomparable pain in my—"

"Play nice, Freddy. After all, I went to a lot of effort to come out to have lunch with you."

Freddy's attention was captured by a man taking the table behind them. Typical. Dmitri hadn't trusted his sister to even meet with her brother without being tailed. "I see you have a new pet goon."

"Yes, Andrei."

Of course it couldn't be a Steven or Andrew. "What happened to the old one?"

"He went missing. Andrei is his replacement." It was the cold matter-of-fact way she'd said it that had Freddy's mind shying away from the possibilities. *Why had she ever got tangled up with Dmitri?* "Now, are we going to sit here talking about my new goon which will no doubt lead to you wanting to discuss my relationship and then me leaving?" Bella waited, daring him to go through with it.

"No. Can't I just want to have lunch with my little sister?"

There was a sourness in the pit of his stomach, the constant ache to save someone who didn't want to be saved.

"You can, but going from how you've been acting lately, I'd say it would be highly unusual." Her lips pursed tartly.

"Such cynicism for one so young. Careful, Bella, dear, it will give you wrinkles." It cheered him to no end when his sister's features smoothed instantly. *Some things never change. She was still as vain as ever.* "You are looking at the proud new owner of a horse."

She blinked, the struggle plain as she tried to keep her face from wrinkling. "When did you buy a horse? Why did you buy a horse?"

"I didn't jolly well buy a horse. I won it. And it even comes with its own rider. You'll never guess who it is."

"The Queen? And what do you mean you won it?"

"The hows aren't really that important." *Trust her to latch on to that piece of information.* "You remember little Carpy Harpy? She was a year younger than you and was always at the pony club camps."

"Little Harper who had a crush on you and who you treated despicably?" This time she couldn't refrain from arching a brow at him. "That Harper?"

Freddy coughed uncomfortably, reaching for his wineglass. This wasn't going quite as well as he'd anticipated. "That's the one."

"Well, as you can tell, I obviously remember her." Bella's mouth formed a perfect O. "Oh, the poor girl. Surely the universe wouldn't be so cruel as to saddle her with you. Do you remember that time you and Landon decided to ride the cross-country course in your pajamas?" She giggled. "And then the district commissioner came out in her dressing gown and chased you both around until she tripped and fell in the mud."

"We were pretending to be steeplechase jockeys. It was

jolly good fun."

"I bet. At least until she made you clean everyone's stables as punishment."

"As I remember, you wouldn't even help us, said you couldn't miss your lessons." *Had they ever been that young?*

"Blimey, I miss those days. I used to love riding so much." She glanced sadly down at where her finger traced a slow circle on the pristine white tablecloth.

A steel weight of despair settled over Freddy in the face of his sister's melancholy. "What happened?" he asked softly.

"I grew up."

"Bella," a deep Russian voice said—the goon from the nearby table. "Dmitri says he has had a change of plans and you are required home immediately."

Icy fury descended over Freddy as Bella's shoulders drooped. "Tell him she's busy having lunch with her brother."

"Bella, is that what you want me to tell the boss? I don't think it will please him."

Freddy slammed his hand down hard on the table, causing nearby diners to stare at him in the sudden silence. "I don't give a fig about what pleases Dmitri."

His sister gave him a tight smile that didn't touch her eyes, and this time it had nothing to do with wrinkles and everything to do with the deep pools of despair that stared back at him. She reached out a cold hand to cover his, giving it a gentle squeeze. "It's okay, Freddy. We can catch up another time. Maybe I can come out and see your new horse."

"That would be good. I love you, Smelly Belly."

"I love you too, Reddy Freddy."

It killed Freddy watching her go. Paying the bill for the wine, he strode from the restaurant. It was time he found a game to take his mind off it before he did something stupid. It appeared his sister had the monopoly on that.

CHAPTER 4

*T*he room was awash with laughter and love. Warm baritones mingled with lighter feminine voices and accents from three different continents.

The smiling faces of friends Freddy considered closer than family surrounded him as he let it all wrap him in a warm embrace and soothe some of the hopelessness from his soul. It seemed like ages since they'd all been together for Cassie's movie premier.

"I can't believe you're going to be parents in a matter of weeks." Cassie's glasses caught the light, glinting as she leaned forward. "And you say you have no idea what you're having?" she probed, clearly not believing Landon and Chora. Freddy thought they were prudent to keep their baby cards close to their chest. After all, anything said in front of Cassie could end up in one of her books.

"You and me both." Landon gazed lovingly down at his wife. "It feels like it's been an age since we found out, and yet the closer it gets, the more I don't feel like I'm ready."

"Imagine how the baby feels, coming out and opening his or her eyes for the first time and seeing who their daddy is."

Freddy smirked at his friend. "Poor child. It's a good thing they'll have Uncle Freddy to look out for them."

"Heaven help them if Freddy is going to be their guiding light." Stirling chuckled, his arm around his fiancée, Cassie.

"Bloody too right," agreed Alistair. "If anyone should be the guiding light in this group, it's me." His lovely Australian wife snorted indelicately beside him. Freddy knew there was a reason he'd always liked Murphy.

"You almost passed out the first time you helped me deliver a calf," she pointed out, brow raised.

"There was a bloody lot of fluids." Alistair turned to his friends in appeal. "The ground turned into a slip and slide of inner mama cow juices."

Freddy gagged at the visual. "Still haven't made a jackaroo out of him yet, I see."

"At this stage, it doesn't seem bloody likely it will ever happen," Murphy sagely noted. "I'm still trying, but his real talents lie in running the Sanctuary. We can't keep up with bookings and they're coming from all over the world."

"I always knew you guys would be able to save those horses, and now that the eco resort is thriving, there's not much your dad can say about it, Alistair." Chora sighed contently. "I do like a happy story."

"Well, Dad still has a bloody lot to say about it, but this time it's more around how I can replicate it elsewhere." Alistair reached for his beer. "And Murphy has a waiting list for the brumbies that she trains for polo."

"I own a horse now too," Freddy casually threw into the conversation.

"Since when?" Chora demanded.

"Since a week ago." He swirled his whiskey lazily around in his tumbler. "It's a stallion."

"What breed?" Murphy's eyes blazed with interest.

"A bay Hanoverian."

"How tall?"

"Very."

"What has he done?" The rest of their friends had fallen quiet during the exchange.

"I'm reliably told dressage."

"Reliably told by who?"

"The rider who came with the horse. I'm led to believe it was some sort of package deal." Actually, now that he thought about it, he wasn't so sure how it all worked. "Rather an attractive little thing, if a little snarky. Turns out I know her from our pony club days."

"Having to deal with you, I can understand why she'd be snarky." Landon laughed.

Freddy raised his glass to his friend. "Steady on, old chap. I'm the very embodiment of charm." He returned his attention to Murphy. "If you like, you can come out and see my horse and then you can ask Harper whatever you want."

Stirling's eyes narrowed at the name. "Carpy Harpy?"

Cassie looked between her fiancé and Freddy, eyes agog. "Oh, I feel a story here."

"Of course you do. You'd find a story on the back of a cereal box if you tried hard enough." Freddy shook his head in mock suffering. "The result of an overactive imagination, I expect." He raised a lazy brow at Stirling. "Yes, that Harper."

Stirling let out a great roar of laughter. It was a trifle overdone, if you asked Freddy. "No wonder she's snarky to you. You were horrible to her when we were kids."

"We," Freddy corrected, enjoying the way Cassie's eyes narrowed at her fiancé. "You were just as bad as I was."

Stirling coughed uncomfortably under his fiancée's regard. "Actually, I don't remember it all that clearly."

Murphy shook her head at their antics. "Back to your offer, I'd love to see your new horse, and I'm bloody intrigued to meet the rider."

Freddy wasn't entirely sure he was ready for it.

~

FREDDY GLANCED around the stable yard as he waited for Harper to notice him and his guests and come rushing over. Everything seemed neat and tidy if rather old. Frankly, he never quite got it about horse girls. Who would want to spend their days covered in grime and out in the elements when there were much easier ways to live? Sure, he'd done the whole pony club thing, but he'd been a child, actively encouraged—one could even say pushed—to have that particular skill added to his social resume. But given a choice, why would one actually choose to do it? He shuddered at the horrifying thought of physical labor.

"I don't think they're going to come over." Alistair smirked at his friend. "Are you sure they know who you are?"

"Oh, this is bloody ridiculous," Murphy muttered before striding over to where Harper and another woman were standing beside a large gray horse, the men shuffling along in her wake. Freddy was fairly confident it wasn't his horse. If he remembered correctly, his was a bay. "Excuse me."

Harper's head jerked, which Freddy thought was a trifle overdone considering he was certain she'd known they'd been standing there the whole time and had chosen to be obstinate. "Yes, can I help you?" *Really?* She knew they were with him.

"I'm here with Freddy, and he tells me he has a horse in training with you."

"Yes, Denny." Harper's gaze flicked guiltily toward Freddy.

"Bloody brilliant. I'm Murphy, a friend of his. Well, actually, my husband is a friend of his and somehow I just ended up inheriting him as part of the marriage." *The dickens, she didn't just say that.*

"You have my commiserations. It might be something you can get a solicitor to help deal with." It didn't help seeing Harper gaze archly at him as she smirked.

Murphy gave a hearty chuckle. "I might have to look into that. Anyway, I have some horses myself."

"That's the most modest way I've ever heard someone describe having nearly one hundred on the property," Alistair pointed out.

"I didn't want to blow my own horn," Murphy replied humbly. "I wasn't sure if I could claim the brumbies or not."

Harper stared at Murphy in stunned silence. "You're that Murphy? From Southern Cross? The Desert Brumbies?"

Murphy reddened under the other horsewoman's regard. "One and the same."

"Carol and I watched the documentary they did on your work with the horses. It's amazing."

"Stirling was great with capturing it all. We were lucky to have everyone come and help us when we needed them. Even Freddy came to the station and did his bit."

The frankly skeptical look Harper cast at Freddy stung a little. "Really?"

"Yes. I helped with the creation of the menu that you will dine on if you ever get the chance to partake of the hospitality of the Southern Cross Station." Freddy had no issues at all with blowing his own horn.

"You cook?" Harper might as well be staring at a two-headed badger from the way she was looking at him.

"Well, Stu, the chef, cooked. But I helped pair all the dishes with a wine menu as well as sampled and compared to what I've tasted at some of the best restaurants in the world."

"So, you ate what someone else made and then washed it

down with some wine. That's what you contributed?" Harper summarized dryly.

"Do you think Chora and Cassie will like her?" Murphy whispered to her husband, loud enough for Freddy to hear. "Because I bloody do."

"I also helped with some wrangling with the jillaroos—or wrangling of jillaroos may be a better description," he conceded, ignoring Murphy's comment.

"You're disgusting." Harper turned to Murphy and Alistair. "I'm sorry to be rude, but I need to ride my next horse if I want to get my work completed today."

Freddy didn't know whether to be amused or irritated that she was actually being nice to his friends while leaving him feeling like he'd been slapped with a wet eel. Maybe he was more of a sick puppy than he'd ever appreciated, because amazingly it was proving to be more stimulating than being at his club. "Have you ridden Denny already?"

"No, I prefer to save him for the last ride of the day." Harper glared at him with hard eyes. "And I like to keep my routine." It was clear she didn't want to budge on it.

"Change is the spice of life and all that." Freddy waved his hands about dismissively. "And since we're here now and not later, I think we would all like to see you ride Denny next."

Carol, the groom who had been brushing the gray horse and until now had chosen to remove herself from the conversation, looked hesitantly between them. "Harper?"

"Fine, put Tippi away for now," ground out Harper. "But only because it would be an honor to have the lady who saved the Desert Brumbies watch me ride." Snatching a headcollar from the rack, she strode away.

"And the man who did the food," Freddy called out after her. He swore that the slap of her boots on the concrete got louder with each footstep. "Maybe we should wait over here," he suggested, guiding them to a bench along the side of the arena.

"Whoa, he's a bloody good-looking horse," breathed Murphy as Denny was led from his stall. Sure, the stallion had a certain amount of presence, but a horse was a horse, especially one that appeared to have used his own manure as a pillow given the large stain on the side of his face.

With brisk assured movements, Denny was quickly put to a state of right and saddled, ready for Harper to mount. After a final check of the girth, she was astride the tall horse, his coat now gleaming a rich mahogany. Freddy could ride a horse well enough to not embarrass himself out at the hunt, but there was something almost sublime about the way Harper sat on a horse. Even when Denny was obviously feeling his oats, she was calm and gracious, redirecting the horse's energy rather than reprimanding him. And once they had warmed up and she asked for the real work, that's when the magic began. It was like watching two souls in perfect harmony as they danced across the sand.

"She is an extraordinarily talented rider," Murphy said, never once taking her eyes from the vision in front of her. "Like, only a small handful of people I've ever met can even come close to her."

Freddy watched the slender girl as the pair did two-time changes across the diagonal, the bay stallion skipping as joyously as any pigtailed schoolgirl could. Murphy was right. Harper was amazing. She took his breath away. Quickly, he shook his head to clear it. Later, he'd have to drown out the thoughts with alcohol—anything to evict the angry, gorgeous dressage rider who seemed to have taken up residence in his imagination.

"It helps that I own a talented horse."

"Only if you can ride it. Those horses, they aren't for everyone, and even professionals can struggle with the sensitive ones," Murphy asserted, this time watching canter pirouettes. The muscles on Denny's hindquarters bunched as he lowered, shifting the weight from his forehand. "If you break the two of them up as a partnership, I'll còme back and hurt you."

"Me?" he protested, all wounded pride. "Why would I do that?"

"Why do you do anything?" Alistair laughed. "Because you're bored and you think it's funny."

Actually, that was rather fair. "As a personal favor, I commit to keeping Harper and Denny together. Happy?" He quite liked the thought of having a reason to keep seeing the dressage rider in her tight breeches with her sharp tongue. Who knows, she might even soften to him. He was, after all, rather charming. Pleased at the thought, he smiled, and coming out of a turn, Harper looked up and saw him. Frowning, she dropped her gaze, her mouth tight as she pushed her mount forward. Maybe she just needed to spend more time in his company.

CHAPTER 5

"*W*hat are you doing?"

Freddy's eyes were artlessly serene as he glanced up from where he stood at Denny's head. Harper had only been gone for a moment for a quick bathroom break and returned to find him mucking around with her—*his*—horse. Carol should have known better than to let him anywhere near the stallion. Speaking of which, where was the groom?

"Calm down, Harper. I come in peace." He showed her the stub of what remained of a carrot, Denny quickly snuffling it from his hand. "I thought Denny and I should get to know each other better."

Harper would have been less dumbfounded if he'd brought the horse a bouquet of flowers. It just wasn't the behavior she'd expected from a jerk like Freddy. *It was a nice gesture.* She quickly hardened her heart. This was the boy she'd had a crush on who had treated her like dirt. The worst bit had been that somehow he hadn't seemed to think it was anything but funny, even though each night she'd cried into her pillow at his meanness.

"He prefers horse cookies."

"All that sugar can't be good for his teeth." Freddy patted the stallion on the neck. "Why don't you go have a nice cup of tea? I believe Carol has put the kettle on."

Was it possible that she'd gone to the bathroom and somehow come out into some weird alternate dimension? "Why has Carol put the kettle on?"

"For a spot of tea, of course. It does seem almost uncivil to not have a cup of tea with cake."

She narrowed her eyes at him. "We don't have any cake."

He bopped her gently on the nose, causing her to jerk back. "Correction, didn't have any cake. But I took care of it. A lovely Victorian Sponge which, if I remember correctly, is your favorite."

Definitely an alternative universe. One where Freddy noticed things about people other than himself. "Carol works for me, not you."

"Do you want me to go tell her you decided she can't have cake? I didn't think you were mean like that. It really is the quiet ones." Harper closed her eyes, counting slowly backwards from ten. Maybe by the time she opened them, he would have disappeared. "Are you okay? You seem a little tense."

Nope, still there. Slowly, she released her breath. "I'm fine, or at least I was until you showed up."

"You don't like cake?"

"This has nothing to do with cake."

"It doesn't? The carrot, then?"

It might actually be possible that Harper was losing her mind, or maybe that was Freddy's sinister plan all along—to drive her insane once and for all. Finish off the job he started all those years before. "NOT. THE. CARROT. NOT. THE. CAKE." Harper pulled herself together, a nerve twitching just under her right eye. "This is my life and I take it very seriously. Based on past experiences with you, that's something you struggle with. It's clear that you don't take owning my horse very seriously."

"My horse."

Her nostrils flared as she fought against her instinct to kick him in the shin. "That leads me on nicely to what I have to say next. I'll send over the schedule for Denny's upcoming competitions for you to sign off on them."

If Harper thought Freddy had a genuine bone in his body, she'd have said he was perplexed as he stared back at her, face scrunched. "Why do you need me to sign off on it? You can go wherever you want." There was almost an angry undertone to his voice. "I'm not your keeper. No one is ever another person's keeper."

This had certainly gotten deeper than she'd anticipated. "Because the entry fees and travel expenses come out of your wallet. You're the owner, you pay. Just like I invoice you for all of Denny's keep, training and any other expenses."

"Blimey, what? Since when?" Freddy looked shocked, like the idea had never occurred to him, which begged the question—what did he think owning Denny entailed?

It really was like dealing with a child. Maybe she'd need that cup of tea and slice of cake when this conversation was over after all. "Since you became the owner, which you like reminding me about so much."

"No one jolly well mentioned anything to me when I won him."

"Maybe they thought you were smart enough to figure it out or at least read the fine print. Obviously, they didn't know you very well." Freddy's eyes narrowed as her barbs hit home. She gloried briefly in the moment before ploughing on. "But now you know. Which reminds me, when I send the schedule over, I'll also make sure to include the current invoice as well."

"Fine. Now, since I've delivered all the gifts I have today, it's high time I leave."

"I thought you'd never offer." *Okay, maybe that was a little petty.*

Turning on his heel, he marched across her yard to his car, muttering about the club being a better choice. *It wasn't even noon yet.* Frankly, she was shocked. But then again, what did she expect from a self-entitled, rich layabout like him?

Herning. Lyon. Stuttgart. Madrid. Salzburg. Amsterdam. Gothenburg. It was a relief to see London at least make an appearance in the schedule Harper had sent over for Denny. Blimey, judging from some of the forms, the horse jolly well even had his own passport. Every item had been meticulously calculated in a handy spreadsheet to show just how much these little jaunts were going to cost him. The figures were a mere drop in the ocean as far as Freddy's trust fund went, but still, it was just a blooming horse. Throwing his tablet away from him in disgust, he stood. Time to find out why his horse couldn't keep his hooves firmly on English soil.

The by now familiar smell of sweet-smelling timothy hay mixed with manure and animal flesh filled his nostrils as Freddy sauntered into the stable yard. As usual, Harper pretended to be serenely unaware of his presence. At least, he thought it was an act. He decided he was being silly—after all, what woman could be ignorant of his enthralling form?

"Harper, a word." He crooked his finger when she flicked a glance over her shoulder at him after her groom whispered something in her ear. Her slight form stiffened. *Maybe the whole finger thing had been an error of judgment.* Not one to look back, Freddy ploughed on. "If you would be so kind."

Stiff, glistening black top boots gave her a distinctive

walk as she made her way over. It might also have something to do with the way she carried herself with a ramrod straightness. "Yes, my lord?" She exaggerated the lord part.

"I don't think we need to stand on formality."

"Then don't order me about like I'm some sort of servant." Her nostrils flared, but otherwise she kept her expression fairly neutral, if slightly on the pinched side.

"It does help if you acknowledge me when I come."

Harper seemed to have developed a rather alarming tic in her right eye. "Acknowledge? When you come uninvited onto my property when I'm trying to work?" She bit off each word.

Freddy waved aside her angry protest. *Women could be so dramatic sometimes.* "It's about your work—or my horse—that I'm here. Why does Denny need a passport?"

"So he can travel." Angry red splotches mottled her cheeks.

"I've seen the places you want to take him. He's going to see more than a nineteen-year-old on a Contiki tour. Is that absolutely necessary?"

She took a deep breath and appeared to be counting. *Strange woman.* "I knew having you as Denny's owner was going to be a pain in my—" She caught herself. "Denny is a horse that is good enough to qualify for the Olympics, with the right opportunities."

Freddy felt like she was being a little overly dramatic. He waved his arm around, gesturing at the other horses in the yard, their heads nodding over stable doors. "What about these, are they good enough?"

"No, and I've been honest with their owners. Denny is a once in a lifetime horse, one that could very well launch me onto the world stage as a rider and trainer." Sighing, Harper raised her eyes skyward. "I know someone up high is laughing at me. For some reason they decided to saddle me with you. That is, if I want to continue riding him." Freddy got momentarily distracted, his head filled with pretty dressage riders in tight breeches and long black boots and all sorts of naughty ideas. Her bitter laugh pulled him back. "They must have a wicked sense of humor."

It suddenly clicked in his mind that she honestly didn't care for him. That it wasn't an act. "Why don't you like me?" *Was there something wrong with the girl?* He knew he was jolly good-looking. The girls were always fighting over him. He had money. Blimey, he even had a title. So, why was Harper all angry frowns and irritated sighs when he was around? She'd been rather lovely to his friends when they'd come out, so he knew she had it in her. *That's it! She's had one fall too many from a horse.*

"I don't care about you one way or the other." Stony eyes stared back at him, challenging him to contradict her.

"Yes, you do."

"No, I don't."

He unleashed what he'd reliably been informed was a devastatingly irresistible smirk. Her face wrinkled as if trying to decipher what she was looking at. *Better put the girl out of her misery.* "That's a shame, since I seem to spend quite a bit of time thinking about you." He let his gaze drop, slowly traveling the length of her. "Especially in those breeches." Satisfied that he'd leave her wanting more, he gave her a jaunty wink. "I'll get my banker to sign off on those expenses." He gave a smoldering look to give her ample opportunity to gush her gratitude. Realizing it wasn't coming—the poor girl was obviously struck dumb by his magnanimity—Freddy decided to leave to let it all sink in. "Make sure you take good care of my horse." With a final smirk, he left.

~

WHAT THE BLAZES had just happened? Harper blinked as Freddy climbed into his car and, gunning it, drove off in a spray of gravel. *Why don't you like me?* There was something in the way he'd said it, like it had genuinely surprised him that someone could dislike him. Her face flamed at what his next words had been, he liked her in her breeches. Was it possible to want to scream and giggle at the same time? Maybe she was still caught up in the leftover emotions of her schoolgirl crush. Was that why it was vexingly flattering? Because grown-up Harper sure as heck wanted to kick the overbearing jerk.

Lining up a luckless piece of straw that had escaped the muckheap ready to send it cartwheeling through the air, she instead sighed, bending to pick it up and return it back to where it had come from. There was no way she could just leave it lying there out of place. If only she could do the same thing to Freddy. A giggle escaped her, rapidly escalating into a full-blown roar at the thought of tossing the irritating billionaire on the manure pile. After all, what was good for the goose was good for the gander. *A girl could dream.*

CHAPTER 6

*T*he baby looked healthy enough, Freddy supposed, wincing as the baby let out a lusty wail of protest as Chora pulled the swaddling cloth away to expose more of him to the assembled friends. "He certainly has a hearty set of lungs on him." Freddy made sure to keep his hands well behind his back. He didn't want the new mother to get any ideas about him holding her new pride and joy.

"The grandparents must be ecstatic that you've produced an heir already," Stirling noted dryly. "Give them a spare next and you'll be off the hook."

"Shush." Cassie jabbed her fiancé in the ribs. *Another one fallen, almost caught now in the matrimonial snare.* Freddy shuddered at how easily all of his friends had forsaken their bachelor ways. Obviously with great women, but still. *Horrifying.*

"The little tacker is bloody gorgeous." Murphy gently touched the baby's cheek with the side of her finger, glancing up at Alistair with a soft questioning gaze. *Oh no, not another one.*

"Imagine if Kelly's little girl and him got married," Cassie sighed. "It would be so romantic."

"Cassie, stop writing the lives of babies who have just been born." Stirling wrapped an arm around his fiancée. "Let them at least get to be toddlers first."

"Edward," Freddy said solemnly to the baby, "you need to ignore your auntie Cassie. The bachelor life is the only life worth living for a chap."

"Oh, hush, Freddy." Cassie shook her head at him. "Stop telling the baby such nonsense. Anyway, the mightier they are, the harder they fall, and I can't wait to watch you fall." She grinned mischievously at him. "I might even write a book about it."

"Don't you dare." Freddy glared at all of his smirking friends. "It's jolly well never going to happen." The ring of his phone stopped him from further uttering denials in the face of his friends' smug certainty. "It's been lovely to have met you, Edward, old chap. Please do stay in touch."

"You better, since you're going to be one of his godparents."

The still ringing phone was forgotten at his best friend's words. He'd just assumed Stirling or Alistair, now respectably settled down, would be chosen. "I am?"

Landon looked down at his weary, beaming wife. Chora gave him a little nod, urging him on. "We were going to wait a little longer before we asked, but now is as good a time as any. Freddy, Stirling, Alistair, Cassie, and Murphy. We couldn't think of better people to guide Edward as he grows into a young man. Each of you are such unique individuals. We know he will grow to be an amazing person."

Freddy listened to his friends agree while he felt blank, amazed, and shaken to his core. Chora and Landon looked at him expectantly. "Of course." Suddenly remembering his phone, he shook it in the air. "I need to return this call. If you'll excuse me. Job well done, Chora."

"I tried." She peered at him closer. "Are you crying?"

Him? Crying? Never. He rubbed at an eye, surprised to find his lashes moist. "I have something in them is all." Before she could ask any more embarrassing questions, he quickly bustled from the room. Now, what had Bella wanted? It was unusual for her to make contact without him having called her at least five times before hand.

"Bella, to what do I owe the pleasure?"

"If that's how you're going to be about it, I can hang up right now." Bella clearly didn't want to be trifled with.

"I just met Chora and Landon's baby." Freddy knew his sister wasn't maternal, which he thanked God for. Imagine her having a baby to the Russian. He shuddered, some things just didn't bear thinking about. She was, however, rather fond of Chora.

"How are the new parents?"

"Disgustingly radiant."

"I bet." A pause, a hesitation as if she was wetting her lips. "I was wondering if I can come out and see your new horse."

Today was the day for shocks, and frankly, Freddy wasn't sure if his heart could take it. "Of course. When would you like me to arrange it?"

"Today? Say, in an hour?" Her words seemed a little rushed even if her tone was still light.

"I'll send through the address. Bella?"

"Yes, Freddy?"

"Is everything all right?'

"Does something have to be wrong for me to want to come out and see your new horse?" The words were now clipped, tightly wound together.

"Of course not. I'll see you there." Gripping the now hung-up phone, he gave a cry of frustration. Knowing you are powerless and accepting it are two very different things.

~

WHEN SHE'D BEEN YOUNGER, Harper had been in awe of Bella. Not only had she been the younger sister of her crush, but there had always been something magnetic about her. Before, she'd been pretty, a hint of the beauty she would become. But now, she was show-stopping gorgeous. It was in times like this that Harper wished she'd spent more time worrying about her appearances growing up and not studying the German training scale.

"Harper, may I give you my condolences." Bella touched her oversized sunglasses with her perfectly manicured hands. "I feel sorry for anyone who has to put up with my brother."

"Be nice, Bella, dear," Freddy murmured, rubbing at the stubble on his jaw. Harper hadn't ever seen Freddy in any state other than cleanly shaven. There was something rather attractive about this scruffier side of him.

"She's being much nicer than I would." Harper smiled warmly at the other woman. "I should also offer my sympathies. I can only imagine what it must be like to be the sister of that man."

White teeth flashed. "I see we are bonded by the shared tragedy in our lives."

Freddy cleared his throat. "Since I'm rather sure all of that was for my benefit, are you quite done?"

Bella sighed. "He's always been so dramatically self-centered."

"I'd hoped he'd grow out of it." Harper's lips twitched as she snuck a cheeky peek up at the subject of their teasing. Standing in the bright light of the stable yard, he good-naturedly took their joking in stride. He still clearly loved his sister, and it was obviously returned.

"So did the family. Alas, it has not turned out to be so." Bella's face sobered as she caught sight of the silent man who had accompanied her, remaining in the car. "It was rather intriguing to discover that Freddy has come into ownership of a rather talented dressage horse, and even more delicious to learn that you were the rider."

Harper felt her ears grow hot as Bella looked from her to Freddy. It wasn't her fault that she'd been lumped with him. "It was unexpected."

"I can imagine, given you probably thought you'd heard the last of him once he'd grown out of pony club."

"I left pony club, I didn't grow out of it," Freddy corrected. "Mother finally conceded that I would be better off pursuing other pastimes. It wasn't like I was going to get any better as a rider anyway."

"That's true," Bella said. "I was the better rider out of the two of us." It had always rankled Harper that Freddy had been given the best ponies, tack and lorries, and yet he didn't appreciate what he'd had. She'd turned up in run-down old horseboxes with wild ponies fresh from the sales.

"Do you still ride?' Bella had been a marvelously quiet rider, so graceful in the saddle.

"My life has taken me further away from it than I would like." The air between Freddy and Bella tensed. Harper was missing something here. "I do miss it."

"If you ever want to ride, I've got several young horses here that you are more than welcome to. A little green, but nice sensible types." Freddy's eyes were bright with approval, more than Harper's simple offer warranted.

"You might regret offering. I'm going to take you up on it and be underfoot all the time." Somehow, there was a brittleness in Bella's words, her body leaning forward.

"I wouldn't have offered if I didn't want you to take me up on it." Harper jerked her head in Freddy's direction. "The only thing I ask is that you try to keep him under control."

This time Bella's laugh tinkled out clear as a bell. "I gave up on that a long time ago."

"Well, I'm beginning to regret setting this up already, for what it's worth." Freddy's expression was tragic and a trifle overdone.

"I don't remember you being a part of it at all," Bella replied tartly. "Harper is the one who offered."

"We're out here because of my horse."

"I'm not riding your horse."

The siblings glared at each other, Freddy shaking his head ruefully. "You're not going to let me take any credit for it at all, are you?"

"No, because then you'd be impossible to be around."

"Are you going to help at all?" Freddy asked Harper, casting his best puppy dog eyes her way.

Harper's tummy did a funny little flip flop. *Stop being silly.* Bella put her arm around her shoulders. "Us girls need to stick together."

"Now I see how it's going to be." And yet somehow Harper didn't think Freddy was as upset as he made out to be.

"And on that note, I need to get home. Dmitri will be expecting me soon." Freddy's face darkened at his sister's words. It was still thunderous, even after he'd walked his sister back to her car and watched her being driven away.

"Thank you, Harper." It struck her that he was genuine.

"For what?'

"I'm worried about Bella, and she won't let me in. She's blooming locked everyone out who cares about her." He kicked out at a stable door, giving a yowl of pain as it connected. Jumping around, he let out a string of curses that would have put a blush on a debutant's face. Good thing Harper was more at home in a stable yard.

She pulled over an upturned bucket. "Here, sit down."

Gingerly, he hobbled over. "Thank you."

"How are the toes?"

"Throbbing." *Throbbing* was not a word that Harper was prepared to hear come from her crush, excuse me, former crush's mouth. A twitter escaped her. "Oh, great. You find my agony amusing."

"No." She felt horrible as another giggle erupted. "It's just, well, you're very dramatic."

"I've been told being dramatic can be rather manly."

"They lied." She giggled even more at his horrified expression. "I'm sorry, I can't seem to stop laughing. She looked down to find him peering up at her intently. Forget flip flops, her tummy was now doing Olympic level gymnastics.

"I like it when you laugh." He looked away. "And I meant what I said before. Thank you for offering to let Bella come out. She always loved riding and maybe ... well, I don't know what I'm hoping for, but I feel better knowing you're here for her too."

This side of Freddy was different to anything she'd thought he was possible of possessing. It challenged her long-held opinion of him in a way that made her uncomfortable. Standing there, looking down at the sunlight glinting off his wheaten-colored hair, Harper felt something shift in her. And she wasn't sure if she liked it or not.

CHAPTER 7

*F*reddy folded his newspaper, making a show of being engrossed in the sports section, crossing his legs as he shifted his weight on his canvas deck chair. *One need not be uncomfortable when spending time at the stables, after all.* For that is where Freddy found himself on this bright and sunny morning. A little too bright if you asked him, and why on earth were the birds singing so loudly? There was a reason Freddy was usually tucked up snuggly in bed at this ungodly hour.

And yet here he was, having taken up the same position he had for the last week as his sister rode under Harper's watchful eye. It was the least he could do, keeping an eye on Bella. Or at least, that's what he kept telling himself. *It had absolutely nothing to do with the sassy dressage rider at all.*

It was a world of order and routine. The horses all fed, watered and mucked out first thing. Rugs changed and haynets filled, horses were led out to fields to frolic and a constant stream of horses were worked by Harper. It was as constant as the clip-clop of the horses' hooves across the concrete. And every day, just as everything centered around the arena, Freddy found his days revolving around Harper. If he was being honest, even the siren call of the clubs and casinos had dulled to a whisper, no longer the roar that had sufficed his entire being. Now it was tart glances over a shapely shoulder or exasperated sighs that he longed for.

"Are you really going to sit there all day again and take up space in my yard?" *Right on cue.*

He made a show of turning the page, rustling the paper. "Just watching my investment."

"Your sister or the horse?"

Freddy hid a smile as his sister gave him a narrow-eyed glare. "I'm hardly an investment," she protested vehemently. *It was surprising she didn't stamp her leather clad foot. Maybe she'd finally outgrown that stage.*

"I couldn't agree more, Bella, dear. You cost a horrific amount of money every time you turn around. If the Russian wasn't pure evil incarnate, I'd almost feel sorry for him."

"Then he must be talking about you." Bella drew Harper into the fray.

Taking the reins of a fresh horse from Carol as Bella finally tied up her mount, Harper flashed an irritated glare his way. *She looked glorious.* "All I know is he's here getting underfoot when I'm working. Most of my owners trust that I know what I'm doing." She left the words hanging, daring him to continue.

"My dear girl, I have complete faith in your ability, but it's refreshing to be around work. I find that I could watch it all day."

"Typical," Bella muttered as she slipped the bridle off her horse's head, giving her mount a rub as he lowered it.

"By the way, is all the matchy-matchy and sparkle stuff there to help you get better or to distract when you're doing badly?" Bella, on her way to the tack room with the bridle and saddle, was either out of earshot or had chosen to ignore him. *That's a little rude.*

"I happen to like it," Harper said through clenched teeth.

Freddy folded his newspaper crisply and set it down on his lap as he looked her over appreciatively. "I rather find myself liking it too. I can think of a few other things I'd like to matchy-match with you." Okay, it wasn't his best line, but his smolder more than made up for it. She wouldn't be able to resist.

A muscle leapt alarmingly to life in her jaw. "Are you always such a lazy, rude pain in the bum?"

Shrugging, Freddy picked up his newspaper again, opening it to the cartoons. "Everyone has to have a hobby, I guess." He swore as she led her horse away that he heard her chuckling. *Stranger things have happened before.*

IF HARPER HAD KNOWN THAT, by inviting Bella to come out and ride, it would also mean Freddy hanging obnoxiously around her yard, she might have seriously reconsidered it. And yet, she found herself waiting for him to make an appearance each morning, retrieving his deck chair from where he'd stashed it in the feed room, surveying the yard for the perfect spot to settle in and read his newspaper. Once he'd finished that, he'd disappear for half an hour, always reappearing with treats and hot drinks for the girls. And it was most certainly not dull when he was around. Even when she wanted to be cranky with him, she'd find a smile creeping over her lips, and she'd have to quickly turn before he could see the effect he was having on her. She didn't want to encourage him, after all.

Having Bella come out and ride had been a revelation. She'd always remembered her as a superb rider, but when she'd been younger, she hadn't noticed the natural feel she had for a horse. In fact, Harper had quickly added a few more of her horses to Bella's ride list. She was almost beginning to feel guilty about not paying her. Checking the girth of the horse she was about to ride, she made a mental note to talk to Bella about it.

It wasn't the only thing that was worrying her about Bella. When she'd first come out for a ride, a rather intimidating man had accompanied her, remaining in the car while she had visited. Each and every time Bella had thus far come to the yard, the same man had come as well. It was a little unnerving.

"What a glorious morning to be alive, and believe me, there haven't been many mornings I've said that," Freddy greeted the yard at large as he sauntered in. "How are you this lovely morning, Carol?"

Carol's cheeks dimpled at him, haynets in each hand. "Excellent as usual. I see you've had your morning coffee."

Freddy held up his tray of drinks. "I'm on my second, so it's only fair that you girls should be too." He held his prize in front of him. "I even got them to add some biscotti this morning."

Harper's mouth began to water. Chocolate biscotti was one of her favorite vices, bequeathed to her by her Italian grandmother. "What flavor?"

"Chocolate. I remember a girl who used to pack a special box of it for every Pony Club Camp." He handed her a cup and slice. "A rather cute girl, if I jolly well remember correctly."

"Can't have been too cute if you kept throwing her in the muckheap all the time." She couldn't keep the bitterness from her voice, let alone her face.

Freddy stared at her, bewilderment plain. "I was just having fun."

"Fun? You call throwing a thirteen-year-old girl onto a pile of horse manure fun? I didn't come from money like you. Those jodhpurs I was wearing was one of two pairs that I owned, and they were the newest, which meant they were the ones I kept for good. I spent the rest of the competitions for the year with stains on them that no amount of soaking removed. I had manure in my hair and everywhere and it was all just a bit of fun to you." She choked over the combination of rage and hurt.

Freddy couldn't have looked more startled if she'd slapped him in the face with a riding crop. He blinked slowly, his mouth opening and closing several times as the blood pounded in her ears. "I guess I never thought about it. I'm sorry."

Blimey, if he didn't seem like he meant it. All the pain and anger she'd stored up against him for years left her in a great gush. It was actually rather freeing to let all the tension go. *Turns out Freddy wasn't mean. He was just a thoughtless, stupid boy.*

"Well, don't let it happen again."

An easy smile played at the corners of his beautiful mouth. "I promise." He looked at her through a sweep of dark lashes.

Her heart fluttered at the puppy dog charm. Flustered, she changed the subject. "Is it normal that Bella always has that man with her? Who is he, anyway?"

"It's normal if you're my sister. And that's her thug, Andrei. The Russian insists that she is always chaperoned."

Harper liked Bella, but she couldn't even begin to fathom the life she led. "That's a little controlling, isn't it?"

"Don't even get me started on what I think about that Russian. He has no right to even breathe the same air as her, let alone control her life."

Sadness settled over her like a shadow. "Not exactly the life you dreamed about for her?"

"Hardly," he said bitterly. "But I'm only her big brother. Why would she listen to me?" For a moment, he studied her intently. "What are your dreams?"

"Win Olympic gold, obviously."

He gave a wry chuckle. "Obviously. What was I thinking? It does sound like jolly hard work."

"It is, and the owner of my top horse makes it harder by trying to fatten me up with biscuits and cake."

His gaze roamed her figure. "Doesn't seem to be working. From where I'm standing, everything is right where it should be."

The cheeky rascal. "Freddy, that's no way to talk to a lady."

"Well, I've known a few ladies, titles and all, and I think you'll find they're rather bawdy. So, you want to be an Olympic champion. What else?"

She was allowed to have more dreams than one? It must be nice to be a billionaire and snap one's fingers and go off in pursuit of another passion. "Fix this place up. Deck it out in all the latest equipment. Solariums, aqua walkers, state of the art riding surfaces and a covered arena. That would be divine."

Freddy's teeth flashed white in his face as he laughed again. "I see the dream still involves horses."

"It's everything to me." She looked at him, caught in a feeling of harmony she hadn't felt with anyone for a long time. "That reminds me, you know, as the owner, you can come and see us compete. I mean at the events in other countries. It might actually be nice to have some support."

Stark vulnerability stared out at her, piercing through her heart. She was surprised that it would mean so much to him to be asked. *To be wanted.* "I didn't know it was a possibility, but I'm not against the idea," he said casually. As if suddenly uncomfortable at exposing himself, he glanced down at his watch. "Look at the time, there's somewhere else I have to be." Setting the drinks down on a nearby bench, he straightened, catching Harper's eye. "Thank you for asking." Before she could respond, he was scurrying across the yard.

Glancing down at her own watch, she saw the time was just after eight in the morning. That surely had to be some sort of new record for him. Harper wondered what else could be so pressing. No one had mentioned a girlfriend. Her lips pursed at the thought of that unpleasant possibility. No, she wasn't jealous. Bella's words from the other day whispered into her thoughts. Her worry that he was drinking and gambling more than was good for him. After all, that was how he'd become Denny's new owner. She looked around her yard sadly. It was full of bright sunlight and fresh air. Her happy place. On the outside, Freddy had it all—title, money, friends. He sure as heck didn't seem to take anything seriously, and yet he didn't really seem like he was that happy at all.

CHAPTER 8

*D*enny stood gleaming on a bed of fresh shavings, the aroma pungent in the air, the bay stallion having been groomed to within an inch of his life. His mane was freshly pulled, and his hooves were immaculate with the farrier having been that morning.

"Well, aren't you the dapper looking chap," Freddy greeted him from the other side of the stable door.

Harper looked up from where she was bandaging Denny's legs. "I should hope so for all the effort he's had put into him."

"How did he go today?" The softly spoken question surprised her.

"Good. Much more relaxed through half-pass." Harper stood and patted the stallion's firm neck. He was in peak athletic condition, ready for the week's worth of travel and competition ahead of him.

"How are you feeling about entrusting him to someone else for a few days?" Freddy asked. Harper chewed her bottom lip, trying not to worry that in the morning they would be parting company.

"Well, it's the only way for me to be in all the places I need to be. Denny will be fine traveling in the lorry to Stuttgart with Carol. As soon as I finish up with the other horses at the young horse competition in Ireland, I'll be heading over." Harper knew he would be in safe hands—Carol loved him as much as she did—but still, Denny was her baby. Hers and Freddy's. She swallowed. *Well, not quite.*

"That's actually something I wanted to ask you about. How are you getting to Germany?"

She looked at him perplexed. How did he think she was getting there? On a magic flying carpet? "Flying."

"Commercial?"

"It's the common way to do it."

"Hopefully you haven't booked tickets yet." His voice was firmer than she was used to, decisive. Harper wasn't going to lie, it was incredibly attractive. "Since I'll be flying over on my private jet, you can come with me."

Harper always struggled with flying commercially, packed in like sardines with other people's smelly feet. She shuddered. Maybe this way she'd get some rest, even a chance for a nap. "Sounds good. Thank you."

"Excellent, I'll let you get back to it, unless there's anything else I can help with." He left the words hanging.

Harper got the distinct impression that he almost wanted her to say she did. "It's all under control. Carol is cleaning the last of the tack, and then we'll start packing the lorry."

"I could help. More than happy to provide the muscle if you need it."

She gave a gentle laugh. "I'm not sure I'd be able to find anything if you helped pack. Trust me, Carol and I have a system, and I'm too superstitious to change it now."

His face turned in a study of self-mockery as he gave her a courtly bow. "I know when I'm not wanted, and as it just so happens, I'm expected at my club. I'll send through details of the flight."

"Thank you. And Freddy?"

He turned, his expression uncertain. "Yes?"

"Just because I don't need your help, doesn't mean you aren't part of the team." She rubbed the back of her arm. "It wouldn't have been the same without you around all the time."

"Like a good luck mascot?"

The way his face lit up, almost like she'd given him a purpose, made her feel ridiculously happy. "Exactly like a good luck mascot."

"Well then. Well, indeed." His back a little straighter than before, he waved goodbye, a spring to his step as he made his way to his car.

Whatever Harper had thought about Freddy before wasn't even close to capturing the complicated little onion he was proving himself to be. The one thing Harper did know was that inside that cocky man about town was a lost little boy.

FREDDY SAT in stupendous luxury as the woman beside him rattled off a list of accomplishments she'd achieved in the several days since they'd parted company that would put even the hardiest to shame. "To finish off with Buddy getting reserved champion four-year-old was just the icing on the cake. All the youngsters did me proud." Harper glowed as she relayed her news to him.

That feeling of accomplishment, success for all the hard work—quite frankly, it was alien to Freddy. It didn't matter if he lay in bed all day, there would still be his butler waiting for him with fresh clothes and food. He never worried about where the money came from. Maximum or minimum effort, it made little difference on the outcome of his lifestyle.

"Does Denny have to be worried that Buddy will overtake him in your affections?"

"Never," Harper responded fiercely. He wondered briefly if she would answer with such passion if he'd asked about himself. He wasn't sure how she'd done it, but Harper had somehow become the bright spot in his otherwise beige existence. Fool that he was, he was too scared to do anything about it in case, like everything, he somehow managed to ruin it. "And now I'm going to try to get some shut eye."

Smiling tenderly, he watched as the tired woman angled her seat backwards, pulling the blanket the hostess had provided her with earlier tighter to her chin. "I promise I'll keep the bed bugs away."

"I know I'm in safe hands," she murmured drowsily, already nodding off.

Poor poppet was exhausted. Freddy settled himself in, not once leaving his station as she slumbered across from him. *I know I'm in safe hands.* His heart clenched at the simple words, spoken so innocently, that rocked his world.

As soon as they'd landed, Harper began to look around for a taxi. Perplexed, Freddy held the door of his town car open for her. "What are you doing?"

"I need to get to the venue to check in on Denny." The way she looked at him like he was a simpleton would have irked him except for the simple fact that Freddy was long used to receiving that look from everyone.

"I'll drop you off on the way to our accommodation. Then when you're ready to leave, I'll give you a number to call and they'll come back to collect you. It's the civilized way to do things. Imagine catching a cab." He shuddered at the ways of the unwashed masses.

She quickly slid past him into the car. "Oh, I usually stay in the lorry with Carol." Harper chewed on her bottom lip. Freddy enjoyed watching her clearly torn between her routine and the potential luxury of a hotel as he joined her. "And I didn't book anything else."

"I booked a penthouse suite. There's room for both you and Carol."

She opened and closed her mouth. "Um, I'm not sure if it's appropriate to share a room with an owner." Flustered, she looked out the window, the dressage venue pulling into view.

"Even with Carol as a chaperone? It's a penthouse suite, Harper, it's not like we're sharing a bed. You'd have your own bedroom." *Why did I have to think about sharing a room with her?* Parts of Freddy were definitely onboard with the idea. He shifted uncomfortably in his seat.

"Well, one of us like to stay on the grounds with Denny, just so someone is on hand at all times."

"Then I guess it sucks to be Carol."

The car pulled to a halt near the entrance of the stadium, official looking people scurrying about. Harper paused, her hand on the door handle, ready to leap to freedom. "I, um, let me talk to Carol, and I'll let you know."

"Harper, if you don't take the room with the nice comfy bed and hot breakfast, you can jolly well bet Carol will. She's not silly, unlike what I'm beginning to think my rider is."

Her mouth formed a perfect O, color flaming to her cheeks. "You did not just call me silly."

Got her. "If the boot—or in this case, riding boot—fits."

Harper narrowed her eyes at him. "I guess it would help my chances at this competition if I got a good night's sleep."

"It would and, now that I think about it, as the owner, I feel that I might have to insist."

The corners of her mouth twitched, setting a ripple of excitement coursing through Freddy. "If you insist."

He pushed himself back into the rich leather of his seat. "If I'd known it was going to be that jolly easy, I'd have insisted on quite a few things earlier."

Harper's giggle tickled his senses as it floated toward him as she stepped lightly out of the car. "Don't get too used to it. Remember, I'm the one who's armed with whips and spurs to get what I want."

Unexpected heat smoldered to life between them. Was she flirting with him? "Promises, promises."

With one last ripple of laughter, she tossed her long braid over her shoulder and, showing her pass to security, disappeared into the stadium, lost to him for the moment. But not for long, he vowed. Harper Ferguson was starting to warm to him. *Jolly well took long enough.*

CHAPTER 9

*T*he excited buzz of the crowd filtered down to Freddy in his private box. It wasn't like sitting at the opera, but it was preferable to sitting with the masses. Last night, Harper had arrived at the hotel in time for a shower and had retired to her room. Any grand plans he might have had to wine and dine her were out the window when she'd informed him that she'd grabbed something with Carol. She'd even jolly well left before he'd gotten up for breakfast, beating his alarm. This was not turning out at all like he had planned.

To be honest, as he surveyed his surroundings, there were a lot more people here than he'd anticipated. Germans apparently loved their dressage. Accepting his first glass of champagne, he settled in. If one had to be here, he might as well make it as enjoyable as possible.

Dutch, English, Danish, Russians, French, Germans and more all entered the center arena, one at a time approaching the judges' box at C before departing toward the top of the arena, anxiously awaiting the siren to sound, marking their start to enter. Then, the tails of the rider's coat swinging in time with their horses, they sashayed down the centerline. Freddy had lost count of how many competitors had performed the exact same test. To be fair, he might have nodded off for several of them, but as soon as he heard the "Next up, Harper Ferguson from England, riding the bay stallion, Denisto II," every fiber in his body became instantly awake.

As Denny trotted toward the judges, his proud neck arched and in a field that included Olympic and world champions, it was clear that there was something special about that horse. A tingle went through Freddy as Harper, face serious, nodded her head sharply before turning the stallion away and heading back to the top of the arena. Everything about the pair oozed confidence. As they entered and began their test, cantering down the centerline before halting and saluting the judges, Freddy shifted his weight to the edge of his seat, champagne forgotten. Having spent weeks watching the two of them prepare, somehow, in this moment, he found them transformed, the great stallion effortlessly answering every question asked of him by his graceful rider as he danced his way across the sand. When they at last performed their final salute, Freddy found that he'd been holding his breath.

With more haste than he'd felt for some time, he bolted to his feet, snatching three glasses of champagne from a passing hostess, and dashed to the competitor's area. Flashing his pass at security, he arrived extremely out of breath as a beaming Harper straightened from hugging her horse, an ecstatic Carol patting his neck.

"Did you see?" Harper asked, straightening up, her face flushed before dismounting gracefully.

"I've never seen anything so beautiful in my life." Freddy could only stare at her, her eyes glowing with pride, her mouth curved in a generous smile. His heart acknowledged the truth of his words. She was spellbinding.

"It was horrible waiting so long, but"—she stressed the word—"it does come with some advantages. I'll know where I'm sitting in scores right about"—she looked up at the digital scoreboard as numbers flashed up—"now." Her eyes filled with tears. "Oh."

Freddy craned his neck around. "I swear those judges jolly well need to get their eyes examined if they can't see a brilliant test when they—"

The words were cut off. "I'm third. Carol, Freddy, we're third heading into the freestyle tomorrow." With a squeal, she wrapped her arms around Freddy, planting a kiss on the startled man. It was the merest of pressures, that in-the-spur-of-the-moment gesture, but one that left him shaken to his core. Even after she'd let him go and had grabbed Carol's hands, the two women jumping around in celebration, he could only stare, rooted to the spot.

Slowly, his immobility captured Harper's attention, and she stopped her leaping around to stare at him, hurt and confusion radiating from her. "Are you disappointed?"

How could she ask that about her kissing him? "I've never been less disappointed in my life. If I was going to be a smidge critical, I would perhaps have wanted it to last longer."

Carol peered around Harper. "She doesn't get to decide that."

"If she doesn't, I don't see who does." Freddy wasn't entirely sure why Carol was getting involved.

"She's right." Harper crossed her arms. "We all do the same test, and from where I was sitting it felt like an eternity, but in a good way." She patted Denny enthusiastically again.

It hit him. She was talking about her current placing. His ears began to burn. There was no way he was going to be able to explain what he really had been thinking. Best to act like it hadn't happened and carry on. "I think third is quite a respectable place."

Harper frowned at him. "Then why didn't you say so?"

"I was distracted." Denny let out a loud snort. "Anyway, shouldn't Denny be getting unsaddled and such?" Freddy made some vague gesture in the horse's direction.

"Yes, yes, keep your shirt on," muttered Carol setting to work.

"Excuse me, Harper Ferguson?" a middle-aged woman wearing sensible shoes and a puffer vest asked.

"Yes?" Harper looked at her uncertainly.

"I'm Beatrice from the Horse and Hound, and if you have a moment, I'd love to ask you a few questions, since you are very much the rider of the hour, appearing out of nowhere."

"I think you'll find that she will be everywhere in the next few months," Freddy said to the reporter. "At least, that's what my accountant has told me."

"And you are?" Beatrice looked questioningly at him.

"I'm Frederick Orstwell. The horse's owner. But I simply pay the bills. This young lady—" Seeing the opportunity, he put his arm around Harper. Maybe it was a mistake, because as soon as he touched her, he lost all focus except for the feel of her. *Maddening.* "Now, where was I?" He gathered his thoughts with great difficulty. "She is the reason Denny is as good as he is. Harper is a generational talent. All the training you see in this horse is her hard work."

She looked up at him, a soft question lurking in the depths of her gaze. Freddy looked away, uncertain if he even knew the answer to her question himself. "Thank you, Freddy."

He cleared his throat. "I'll leave you ladies to it. I think a drink is in order to celebrate. Now, if you'll excuse me." At their agreeance, he bolted, uncomfortably aware of how close to dangerous territory he'd gotten. *Nothing a good strong drink and maybe some cards couldn't fix.* Pulling himself together, he slipped outside to his waiting town car. *Yes, that was just the ticket.*

~

FREDDY HAD BEEN odd ever since she'd finished her first test. Warming up for her freestyle, it was most definitely not the time to be thinking about that man. Frustrated, Harper put her leg on a little firmer than she'd intended for the canter pirouette, Denny swishing his tail in protest. The steward ushered her forward. Taking a deep breath, she plastered her game face on. *Definitely not the time at all.* Pushing him as far as possible from her mind, she gathered the stallion up.

"Let's go show them what we can do," she whispered to her horse. "Again."

~

"I CAN'T BELIEVE IT. I know there are areas we need to improve on—he carried way too much tension in the free walk. But to finish in third. I can't even deal with it." Harper stopped her rambling to look across the table at Freddy, the man polishing his trophy. "Do you need a moment over there?"

"Huh?" He straightened his hunched shoulders. "Why didn't you tell me I would get a trophy? I rather enjoyed standing there being presented with my prize, but it's best to tell a chap. You know, to warn them."

"I didn't think it would be such a big deal to you." As far as she could remember, he'd won plenty back in their pony club days.

"Well, it is." He peered at her, and her heart clenched at

the vulnerability naked in his gaze. "This might surprise you, but I needed this." His lashes lowered over his eyes, shielding them from revealing more. Freddy ran his hands through his hair. "And I didn't even know how much I needed this—all of this—until it happened."

Harper felt her breath catch in her throat. He didn't mean just the trophy. He meant her, too. She was sure of it.

Freddy cleared his throat. "What's the end game with Denny?"

Harper almost got whiplash from the abrupt change in conversation. "I guess what I said when you first became his owner. This horse is good enough to get to the Olympics." She stared down at where her fingers traced a circle on the pristine white tablecloth, her empty plate waiting to be cleared. "And I'm good enough." She wasn't sure why she needed to add that. Somehow it felt like she needed to claim it for herself. Or maybe she wanted him to acknowledge it. To hear him say it to her.

"So, how do we jolly well get there then?" Freddy stretched his hand out to lightly clasp hers. Harper's breath hitched. *Was it his touch or his words?* "We?" Her voice was unsteady as she locked eyes with him.

"Yes. We. I assume that's satisfactory to you since you want to take my horse to the Olympics." He held up his trophy. "Do I get a gold medal as an owner?"

"No." She found herself distracted by the warmth of his skin on hers. *Stop it, its only hand-holding, nothing to get silly about.*

"That's a little disappointing." He pulled a face of exaggerated dismay. Harper almost mirrored it when the waiter appeared to clear their dishes, causing Freddy to release his hold. "You didn't answer my question, though. How do we go about getting our horse to the Olympics?"

"We plan and train and work even harder. Throw in lots

of money to pay for everything, and a lorry full of luck and we have a chance." Her words might be flippant, but the band of steel running through them fastened her determination firmly to her intentions.

"I've always done rather well with luck. She seems to favor me." Freddy signed for their meal and handed the receipt back to the waiter. "Look where it's got me so far, sitting in Stuttgart with one of the most exciting dressage riders to explode on the scene for years."

Harper could feel herself flush, even though she knew he was joking. She laughed when he waggled his brows at her. "You can stop doing that anytime soon."

Freddy pushed back his chair and, closing the distance between them easily, held his hand out to her. "Only if you promise to smile more."

"I smile plenty," she replied affronted.

Freddy looked down at his waiting hand and back to her expectantly. Harper wondered how such a gorgeous man could have such a boyish charm. "Let me rephrase that. How about you promise to smile more around me."

Relenting, she accepted his hand and rose, falling easily into step as they left the restaurant for their room. "I think I might be able to see what I can do." Her lips quirked as he peered at her from the corner of his eye.

"Is that a yes? And is that a—" He stopped to stare intently at her. "I think it is. Harper Ferguson, are you actually smiling at me?"

She clasped a hand over her mouth to stop the giggle spilling out from her without success. "Maybe."

Freddy turned until he was facing her fully, his gaze traveling her face, searching her eyes intently. Harper, by no means blind to his attraction, felt a lurch of excitement within her as he gently pulled her hand away from her mouth. She could have sworn she heard him mutter, "Fortune favors the brave." While she still pondered what on earth that meant, he stepped forward, clasping her body tightly to his. Harper could feel his uneven breathing on her cheek as his lips claimed hers hungrily. She quivered at his mastery as she lost herself to his touch.

Harper let out a small cry when he released her, the loss of his touch painful. She could only stare at him, knowing in the very depths of her soul that everything had changed in that instant, that somehow there would be no turning back. Freddy returned her gaze with a determined set to his mouth.

"I'm jolly well not going to apologize. I don't regret kissing you." He rubbed the back of his neck. "The only thing I regret is not doing it sooner."

"It's actually the second time you've kissed me today." Harper's lips curved as she couldn't resist teasing him.

"You kissed me, and I'm not even sure that can be classed as a kiss now that I think about it."

"But this one now qualifies as a real kiss?" She knew there was more than a hint of challenge in her words.

"I say, since you're clearly in doubt, it's best I do a proper job of it."

Thrilled, Harper found herself once again in his warm embrace, savoring every minute of his lips on hers, her senses reeling. Tomorrow, she would worry about training and schedules. Tonight, she wanted only to live for the now —in this man's arms.

CHAPTER 10

*L*yon, Madrid, Salzburg, Amsterdam, Gothenburg. It was a constant whirl of shows and countries with breaks back to the yard back home for Denny and Harper to regroup and recover before getting back on the rollercoaster again. For Freddy, having had no real purpose in life for so long, it was a revelation. Here with Harper and the horses, he was needed. But more than that, he was wanted. Just him, nothing else. That didn't stop him from spoiling her.

"What on earth have you done now?" Harper demanded as he climbed down from the horsebox.

"I thought it was time to upgrade, and I was told there was nothing better than an Oxley horsebox." He paused, momentarily doubting his information before shrugging it off. It had cost enough to be true.

"But we have a horsebox here already and it still does the job." Harper shook her head in bewilderment.

Carol, on the other hand, already had her nose in the living quarters door. "Be quiet, Harper, and thank the nice man."

Freddy smirked at his stubborn girlfriend. "Listen to Carol and thank the nice man."

She rolled her eyes skyward but did what she was told— and a jolly good job of it too. Freddy had no complaints about the kisses she lavished on him.

"Gross. I didn't come here to have to see you two sucking faces," Bella groaned, her goon shadowing her.

"I suggest you leave then, because I'm never going to stop kissing this woman," Freddy murmured, his lips still pressed against Harper's. Releasing her reluctantly, he scrunched his brows as he surveyed his sister. It was a warm day, and yet his sister had arrived at the yard in long sleeves, the collar pulled tight around her neck. Her ever-present sunglasses were on with her hair framing her face. It seemed like overkill to Freddy, but Bella had always been rather protective of her complexion. If you asked him, she took the whole idea of being an English Rose a little too far.

"Have you seen the new aqua walker?" Carol asked, emerging from the ramp of the lorry. The groom didn't appear to have any complaints about the gifts that kept appearing at the yard.

"The aqua walker?" Bella glanced back toward her brother.

"Yeah, it's a treadmill for horses that fills up with water so they can do hydrotherapy. Apparently, all the cool horses have them."

"I think Freddy is on a mission to completely revamp my poor little yard," Harper said, breathlessly looking lovingly up at him. His heart twisted in a painful knot, fearful it wasn't worthy of the way she gazed at him. "The solarium, heated rug racks, red light therapy rugs, the new rubber pavers on the concrete. The latest he wants to do is put in a covered arena."

"Well, I have to do it this way since you jolly well won't let me just move you to a new state of the art purpose-built facility." He cherished her a little more because she hadn't jumped at it, clinging instead to the sentimentality of her yard.

Harper batted his arm. "I like it here. There are memories."

Freddy pulled her in close, setting her to fits of giggles when he gently kissed the tender part of her neck. "I can help give you lots of new memories, if that's the only thing stopping you."

"I don't know how you put up with those two," Bella grumbled to Carol.

The groom hid a smile. "She pays me well."

"I'd ask for more." Bella sighed. "And it still wouldn't be enough."

She might have said more, but Freddy had his hands full, showering kisses over the giggling woman who had captured his heart. And right now, nothing was more important than that.

"WE'RE DOING WHAT?" Harper wasn't sure she'd heard right.

"Isopoding. Or at least, that's what I think it's called when you're doing it. The contraption is called an Isopod, at least." Freddy held out the champagne bottle and waggled it at her.

Obediently, Harper held her glass to be topped up. "That still doesn't answer my question, Freddy."

He set the bottle down on the table beside him and settled back on the couch, pulling her into him. It was nice to snuggle on the sofa at the end of a long day. If Harper was honest, it was even nicer having supper prepared by a butler with no worry about preparing or cleaning up. "I was talking to my friend, Landon, the other day about our preparations, and he said that a few sessions in an Isopod could be helpful. You go lie in a tub of hot salty water, some music plays, they turn off the lights and you float. Look, I don't really understand it either, but I think it's worth a go, so I've booked you in."

She liked the way he said *we*. "I'm amazed you didn't just order one for the yard."

He kissed the top of her head. "Would you like one?"

"I don't even know if I like it yet, and even then, I'm sure I could just arrange sessions as I need them." Freddy was starting to get a little too trigger-happy with purchasing things for her.

"Or I could get one installed here," he suggested. "Or anything else you might want here." He left it hanging. Was he suggesting she move in? Harper marveled at the sense of contentment that flowed through her at the thought of living with Freddy.

"Lord Orstwell," the butler intoned. "Dinner is served." *Just when it was starting to get interesting. Maybe having a butler wasn't the bee's knees after all.*

THE FIST inside her brain tried to beat its way out of her skull. Even the act of breathing made her skin crawl painfully. Gratefully, Harper patted Denny's sweaty neck, not sure how she'd manage to guide him around his test. She closed her eyes, bracing herself for the jarring impact that would make it feel like her brain was splintering apart as soon as she dismounted. Knowing putting it off wasn't going to change the outcome, she gritted her teeth and committed to it.

A gasp of agony escaped her at the fresh torment, and she leaned into her horse, trying to breathe, his familiar odor soothing despite her distress. "What's wrong, Harper?" Freddy's voice sounded a mile away.

"She has a migraine," Carol said from somewhere near Denny's head.

"Has she taken anything for it?"

"Not allowed under the anti-doping policy," Harper murmured, sparks of pain igniting as she spoke the words.

"Then why did you ride? Actually, how did you even manage to remember your test?" Freddy gently pulled her away from her horse, tenderly holding her as he rubbed the back of her neck.

"Because the selectors are here." Harper was grateful when Carol spared her from having to reply. "And there's no way we would travel all the way to Madrid and have her not compete. It's also probably why she has the migraine. She always gets them when she's under a lot of pressure, and boy, has she been heaping it on herself lately."

Harper closed her eyes, giving in to the steady, rhythmic pressure of Freddy's fingers at her neck. All she wanted to do was curl up in a ball and pass out, anything to escape her misery. "You need to relax." She could feel the warmth of his breath near her ear as he whispered to her. Even in her agony, a shiver ran through her at the intimacy. "I happen to be a world leading expert on how to be loose. Bella will vouch for me."

"I think you've improved," she mumbled, still not opening her eyes.

"Enough is jolly well enough." Suddenly, Harper was lifted into the cradle of Freddy's arms. "I'm taking her back to the hotel." She buried her head into the corded muscles of his chest, closing everything else out as she gently swayed with each step he took, propelling them toward sanctuary. She was safe. Freddy had her.

"HARPER?" The gently insistent voice parted the curtains of sleep that held her in its dark embrace. "Sweetheart, I wouldn't wake you if it wasn't important."

"I'm awake," she opened her eyes groggily, squinting at the light stabbing at her eyes.

"I have Lionel Steward on the line. The chap told me that he's one of the selectors."

Harper's eyes flew open, all traces of drowsiness fleeing as she reached for the phone Freddy held in his hands. "Hello, this is Harper speaking."

"Excellent. I'm so glad I've managed to get through. Your groom mentioned you were feeling unwell," the cut-glass English voice said on the other end. The voice had a dusty quality, like its owner was reluctant to use it.

"A slight headache, nothing major." Even as she spoke, it still felt like her brain had been beaten to a pulp by a mallet.

"Jolly good. The other selectors and I have been keeping an eye on you and your horse. You made rather an impression on the dressage world in a very short period of time."

"It's funny, I've spent years working hard to be an overnight success."

"Many do and still don't reach the level of success that your current trajectory seems to have you on course for." He paused. "As such, you've been identified as an emerging talent and have been added to the squad for the European Championships."

Harper was too stunned to do more than nod before remembering she was on the phone. At the doorway, she could see where Freddy had taken a few steps back to give her the pretense of privacy. He looked at her questioningly. "It's an honor."

"It's a responsibility, and you are by no means guaranteed

to make the team. I suggest you don't drop the ball now and continue with the success you've been having. The selectors will be in touch with details around squad training and commitments." Clearly having used his word limit for the day, Lionel hung up.

"Well? What was that about? You look like you've been hit with a rubber chicken." Freddy stalked back into the room, stopping directly in front of her.

Harper let out a slightly hysterical giggle. "A rubber chicken?"

"Yes, now what happened?"

"That was one of the dressage selectors." The enormity of the situation hit her, tears blinding her eyes and choking her voice. "I've been selected for the British Dressage Squad."

Though blinded by her emotions blurring her vision, she felt the mattress dip as he sat beside her, his nearness comforting as he wrapped an arm around her. "This is a happy moment."

"It is," she sniffled.

"You deserve this." He pulled her in closer until her head rested in the nook of his shoulder. "I believe in you, and until I met you, it had been a very long time since I'd believed in anything." Freddy cleared his throat. "You have a gift, and people have only just seen the tip of what you can do. I'm jolly well grateful that somehow, I'm lucky enough to be along for the ride."

"Everything you've done—getting all of the equipment to help make sure Denny is in fighting fit condition, the new lorry—it's what helped us get here." She looked up at him through tear-spiked lashes, her heart lurching madly. "But the biggest thing has been you." Harper swallowed the lump in her throat. "If you'd told me when I was in that manure heap all those years ago that I would be thanking you for being you, I'd have said you were bonkers." She placed her hand lightly on his chest, a thrill racing through her when she found his heart hammering madly.

Freddy tenderly closed his fingers around her hand. "I feel like I'm bonkers for thinking that maybe you feel about me the same way I feel about you."

Her pulse quickened at the question in his words. "I think I do."

As if her words had released him, he turned her face until it was inches away from his own, his lips hovering, waiting. "That's enough for me." Then he sealed his vow with a kiss.

That's enough for me too ... for now.

CHAPTER 11

*A*nother week, another country, this time the FEI dressage circus had rolled up to Amsterdam. Freddy watched as Harper worked Denny in the warmup arena. He couldn't help smiling to himself at the perfectly coordinated picture they presented. His girlfriend was still a firm believer in sparkles and matchy-matchy. The ring of a phone pulled his attention away from the harmonious pair. Baffled, he looked at the blank screen before remembering that he'd been left in charge of Harper's phone as well. Fishing it out, he felt a twinge when he saw Bella's name flash up. It had been weeks since she'd last tried calling him. She was perfectly civil when they saw each other out at the stables, but she hadn't tried contacting him the way she used to. *Obviously, she had no such qualms calling Harper.*

"Hello, sister dear." He answered the phone.

A slight pause. *Good, he'd surprised her.* "Hello, Freddy. I wasn't expecting you to answer Harper's phone."

"What can I say? We're at the answering each other's phone stage in our relationship."

"Cute. Can you get her to give me a call when she's available?"

The pain at her curt preparation to end the call hurt. "I will. How have you been, Bella?"

Another pause, a slight cough. *How had his sister gotten so lost to him?* "I've been good, Freddy. It's been wonderful seeing how well Harper and Denny are doing."

"They deserve it. She has a training camp coming up at the end of the month for the British Squad. I have every confidence she will impress them."

"I'm quite sure she will. I would actually like to come over and watch her at the European Championships if she does."

Bella could find time for Harper, but not for him. The sting of rejection set fire to jealousy, and he pushed back with ammo he knew would hit home. "I'm amazed Dmitri would allow it. Does he even know you're calling?"

"Dmitri is away on business at the moment, but he is eager to accompany me."

That will be the day. "I didn't know he liked dressage. Is this the softer side you keep telling me about?"

"And this is the side of me telling you to mind your own business."

"You're my little sister."

"And I'm a grown woman."

Freddy gave a short, ugly bark of humorless laughter. "Then act like it. Why do you let him treat you the way he does? I'd love to know, Bella, what hold does he have on you? If you're so grown up, leave him. Come home. If you don't want to be alone, you can always stay with me."

The silence stretched. When she finally answered, it was with an infinite sadness. "You don't understand. I'm not a little girl who you can protect from getting bruised anymore. If you love me, you need to stop nagging at me."

"I can't do that, Bella." The pain from the fact there was nothing he could do drove a stake into his heart. "I love you."

"I love you, Freddy, but I need you to leave me alone. Get Harper to call me." The phone line went dead.

Anguish ripped through him, and he closed his eyes feeling utterly miserable. "Surely it wasn't that bad?" Harper asked.

Freddy opened them to find her smiling down at him from Denny, the great bay stallion covered in sweat from his exertions. "There's somewhere I need to be. Don't wait up for me tonight."

A glazed look of shocked hurt spread over Harper's face that, only moments before, had been beaming. "I'm sorry, what did I miss here?"

"Nothing, but I've been neglecting some other aspects of my life while I've been focused on your dreams." *Why had his tongue turned so mean?*

She swallowed, a sheen of tears glistening in her eyes. "I never asked you to do any of this."

"I need to go." He was only making things worse. Like a wounded animal, he wanted to maim everyone around him. Whirling about, he turned and fled before he could drive away another person he loved.

THE OILY STAIN was like a skin on the surface of the water as Harper rinsed her cloth clean. Disgruntled when she caught her own angry reflection, she slapped it away, causing ripples to splash against the side of the water bucket. "You know what makes me mad?"

"Too much mustard on your sandwich?" Carol said with a straight face.

"No. Well, yes, I don't like lots of mustard. It drowns out

all the other flavors. But that's not what I was going to say, and stop trying to make me laugh. I'm in too foul a mood for you to succeed." Harper dug her cloth into the tin of saddle soap before attacking her tack.

"Challenge accepted," Carol managed with only the slightest glimmer of a smirk. "But what makes you mad, Harper?"

"Everything's going fine, then the next minute he completely shuts me out. I don't even know what bee he's got in his bonnet, and then he goes and has a dig at me. Like I deserve to be treated like that." She could feel the heavy weight of the negative energy pressing down on her. "I bet he's out there somewhere getting drunk and gambling."

"Maybe he'll win you another horse." The smile slipped from the groom's face when she saw Harper's reaction to her joke. "Too soon?"

"Most definitely too soon, and you might as well give up. I'm not going to be coaxed into a better mood."

"So, you're committed to it then? The mood, I mean," Carol asked, looking slightly past her. "Because if you are, I must admit to feeling conflicted."

Harper rubbed harder at her saddle. "Why are you conflicted? I'm the one who's got drama going on."

"Because I'm about to have a front row seat to the drama, and I'm conflicted whether I want to stay and watch or get the heck out of dodge."

Harper spun around at Carol's words, hating that her heart beat faster when she saw Freddy only yards away from them. "You could have said something sooner," she hissed.

"I said something as soon as you gave me the chance to get a word in." The other woman set her sponge down. "You know, I think I might go check on Denny."

"You get back here," Harper muttered, not ready to be alone with the man who had caused her piqued mood.

"Hello, Freddy. Goodbye, Freddy." Carol brushed her hands clean on her jeans in preparation for her escape.

"Hello, Carol." Freddy looked worse for wear, the top two buttons of his shirt undone and his hair tousled. Blearily, he watched the other woman depart. "Was it something I said?"

"It wouldn't surprise me. You seem to have a knack of offending people today." She knew her tone was shrewish, but she didn't care that he knew how she felt. He'd been the one who had been the jerk.

"I deserve that." He turned over a bucket and sat down beside her.

"Yes, you do." Harper wrung out the rag in her hands with gusto, causing Freddy to wince. "If it happens again, I'm going to get you in the balls."

He looked uncertainly at her, as if there was a chance she was joking. "That's a bit extreme, don't you think?"

"So is you flying off the handle at me like that for whatever reason I still don't know. I think I'd only have to kick you once for you to think twice about ever doing it again." Amused, Harper noticed that Freddy's hands protectively cradled those treasured parts of his anatomy.

"I think the stakes are high enough that I promise to never do it again." He reached into his pants pocket and pulled out a velvet case. "I already dropped off Denny's present for being a jerk when I stopped by his stall looking for you. This is your one."

Harper took the small box from his hand and opened it, letting out a gasp at the magnificent piece of jewelry inside. "It's beautiful."

"I was going to buy you a necklace, but then I thought that this would be better." He looked down at the gleaming brooch nestled inside on a bed of red satin. "I thought you could wear it on your stock when you compete."

She could only nod as she stared down at the piece, not

trusting herself to speak. Harper swallowed hard. "It looks expensive. I'm scared I might lose it if I wore it."

"I picked it because it has seven European cut diamonds, and I've always found seven to be my lucky number." Freddy smiled tentatively at her. "Please wear it. I'd hate to think of it kept safe somewhere no one would ever see it."

Harper was mesmerized by the extraordinary sparkle and brightness of the icy-white diamonds, the largest—the center stone—dazzling against a captivating geometric design accented by contrasting foliate motifs all set in platinum. "That's a lot of diamonds."

"A total of 5.85 carats."

It was clear he wanted her to use it and cherish it and it was a truly gorgeous piece of jewelry. "I promise to wear it for good luck each time I compete as long as you tell me what got you acting like a jerk so much that you had to buy it for me to apologize."

There was a pensive shimmer in his eyes, and her heart twisted. Maybe he wasn't going to tell her after all. "Bella called your phone and wanted to speak to you. She hasn't called me in a while. And then we had words." He spoke with a light bitterness, shaded with pain.

"I'm sorry it hurt your feelings, but maybe it's good that she feels like she can talk to me. That she has a friend who cares."

"She has a brother who jolly well cares," he exploded, pounding his fist into his thigh.

"I know you want to protect her, but the more you pick at her about her relationship, the more you're going to drive her away." Her chest constricted when his face fell. "She's a grown woman. She needs to be ready to leave. You can't make her and, until then, all you can do is be there for her. And I mean by not judging her. Truly be there for her. You need to let her make her own mistakes."

His cry of pain as he seemed to crumple from within tore at her. Harper moved closer to wrap her arms around him. "But what if it kills her?"

Harper closed her eyes against the sting of tears. "Bella's strong. She won't let it get to that."

As she gently rocked him back and forwards as if soothing a child, she could only pray that she was right.

CHAPTER 12

*H*arper's face scrunched up in concentration, as she read the piece of paper. In the arena just in front of her, Bella was on one of the young horses, face serious as she rode under Carol's supervision. To one side, her ever present goon stood, arms folded as he stood guard over his boss's girlfriend. Freddy sat quietly in his chair, waiting for her to finish her perusal. "Well?"

"It has a lot going on," she allowed, worrying her bottom lip. As soon as they'd got home, Freddy had commissioned a new freestyle choreography and it was a huge step up from their last one.

"Do you want to have Carol call it for you with the music and see how it feels? The company that created it did the last Olympic gold medal freestyle." Freddy, bless him, had done his research before laying his money down.

If she could pull it off as the harmonious exhibition it was intended to be, it was a world winning performance. It was that fine line between disaster and triumph that set her teeth on edge. "I know it's meant to be as difficult as possible without stressing the horse, but the composer clearly doesn't have the same issues about doing it to the rider."

"Sometimes to reach one's true potential, you have to be well and truly pushed outside of your comfort zone." Freddy's steady gaze bored into her with silent expectation. *He believes I can do this.*

Resolve set, she couldn't resist teasing him first. "Did you read that in a life coach book?"

"Actually, it was in *How to Be the Best Armchair Coach You Can Be for Your Girlfriend.*" There was something warm and enchanting in the humor sparkling from him. "And I'm jolly good at the job. You won't believe the section it has on how to take their mind off things." He tapped his chin thoughtfully. "Which reminds me, I need to get a feather."

"A feather?" Bella asked as Carol and her made their way over. "Actually, I don't believe I want to know."

"Smart girl," Carol complimented, as she held the horse steady for Bella to dismount. "There are some things that are best left unknown." Bella's graceful dismount was marred at the merest hint of a wince as she landed.

"Are you okay?" Harper asked.

Bella rubbed at her side and Harper couldn't help but notice her usually immaculate manicure now had two nails that looked torn, noticeably shorter than the rest. It was possible she'd done it while riding, but somehow, Harper didn't think so. "Just a little stiff this morning, I must have slept funny."

A muscle worked in Freddy's jaw as he gave his sister a hard stare. Clearly it sounded as fake to him as it did to her. He looked over at Harper, muted anger and pain shimmering, but he held his tongue. Harper knew how difficult it was for him, and her heart twisted at his helplessness.

"I meant to ask, how was the first team training day you

went to?" Bella asked a little too brightly. *She was definitely hiding something.*

"Good. I was nervous, but once I got over that, it was so worthwhile."

"I should jolly well hope it was worthwhile given how serious everyone took themselves," Freddy said. "A few of them were a right bunch of snobs, and I should know since I was raised around nobility. I don't think there was a lord or lady to be found in the lot of them." He paused as he thought something over. "If we get married, you'll outrank them all."

Harper almost died on the spot at his casual comment, making a strangled noise. Bella looked between the two of them in amused contemplation. Carol, for her part, nodded in approval. She clearly liked the idea. "I'm not sure that's a reason to get married," Harper finally managed to get out.

"No, but it would be satisfying getting them to call you Lady Orstwell." He gave her a look that promised all sorts of things she wasn't ready to contemplate. Things he clearly had. "Maybe later, over wine, I can give you a few more reasons."

Harper felt completely out of her depth. They'd never spoken about their relationship past the fact that it felt right. Somehow, she'd never considered what the next step might be. Flustered, she looked down at the piece of paper she still held in her hand, smoothing out where she'd crumpled it. "I think it's time I try to ride this."

"But Denny isn't even saddled yet," Carol pointed out, untacking Bella's horse.

"I know how to get a horse ready," Harper replied, grabbing a halter. She was about ready to run the next person over who stopped her. "Now, if you'll excuse me, I'm going to do just that." With quick strides, she escaped.

"Harper?" Freddy called.

"Yes?"

"When you're finished, we can have that wine and I'll give you some of those reasons. I promise I'll have a feather by then as well."

Her stomach quivered at the promise in his words. Not knowing what to do, she did the only thing that made sense. She fled to the safety of her horse's stall.

FREDDY IDLY STROKED the feather between his fingers as he waited for Harper to arrive. For the last few days, he hadn't been able to shake an increasingly uneasy feeling he'd had. He didn't even want to think about what he suspected was happening to Bella. Since he'd taken Harper's advice, she'd seemed to almost breathe a sigh of relief when he was around, no longer looking to avoid him. He hated that he couldn't do anything, but at least his sister wanted him to be around again. It was a small win, and he comforted himself with the thought that he would be close if she needed him.

But this feeling was like catching something out of the corner of one's eye and then, when you turned to look at it fully, there was nothing there. The feeling of always being watched, the hairs on the back of one's neck standing against the eerie presence. There were times when he was driving out to Harper's yard that he swore the car behind him was following him, only for it to turn off at the last moment. He shook his head at the folly of his own imagination. If he told Harper, she would think he was losing the plot and, what's worse, he could potentially be the cause of her losing focus. No, for now he would keep it to himself.

"Freddy, I'm sorry I'm late. The battery in my car was flat and I had to call a cab." Harper glided into the room in jeans and a cashmere sweater, fresh-faced as a daisy. She bent down and kissed him, sunshine and hay teasing his senses.

He took a deep breath, fighting against the spasm of anxiety that gripped him. *You're being silly, old chap. Flat batteries happen.* "You should have called. I could have come and got you."

"Oh, I didn't want to be a bother." She waved away his offer, sitting down beside him and reaching for the glass of wine he'd poured for her earlier.

"I could have sent the town car," he insisted.

Harper gave him a smile that set his pulse racing. "I promise I'll call next time." Her brows lowered together as she caught sight of what was in his hands. "Is that a feather?"

Freddy gave her a wicked smile of his own. "Yes, and I believe I have a promise of my own to keep." Enjoying the way she bit down nervously on her lip as a delicious giggle escaped her, he pulled her close. "And I always keep my promises."

CHAPTER 13

The gravel crunched underfoot as Harper ran, Denny trotting smartly alongside her. Once she reached the end, she stopped and turned her horse before repeating the process back toward the selectors. There was a strange buzzing in her ears as, heart pounding with nerves, she came to a complete halt. "Thank you, Ms Ferguson, that is all we need."

The abruptness was jarring. The vet smiled at her kindly. "You've done a right smart job of presenting your horse. He looks fit as a fiddle."

"We'll announce the final team shortly." Lionel made a shooing motion like she was a horsefly bothering him. Feeling like it was all a little anticlimactic, Harper gave a half wave that only the vet returned before she glumly led Denny back to the stables.

"Well?" Carol asked, her entire being leaning into the question.

Wasn't that the million-dollar question. "Don't call us, we'll call you kinda deal." Harper felt completely drained. Maybe it had been naïve, but she'd assumed that she would know one way or the other today.

Freddy pulled out a Union Jack emblazoned hip flask—*that's new*—and took a swig before offering it to Carol. Harper's brows shot up in surprise when the groom took a hearty gulp before passing it over to Harper. She quickly waved it away. Today was not the day to get tipsy. "If they want the strongest team, then you'll be on it." He took his flask back and had another drink. "Politics aside, of course."

That's what worried her. It wasn't enough to be good or have a sound horse, you also had to play the games the selectors insisted on putting their riders through. Harper wasn't sure she had the stamina for it all.

"Harper Ferguson?" a plain young woman asked, holding a package in her arms.

"Yes?"

"Lionel asked me to give this to you and say congratulations." Dimples appeared as the woman smiled, leaning closer. "I think he likes you. You're the only one he's taken pity on and put out of their misery."

Somehow, Harper doubted it, but she took the proffered parcel anyway. Staring down at it, she marveled that it wasn't larger. It held one of her lifelong dreams, after all.

"Well?" Freddy asked. "Are you jolly well going to open it and put us out of our misery?"

"She doesn't have to. We already know." Carol grinned at Harper. "Don't we?"

"I can't imagine they would give me anything except a 'thanks but no thanks' if I didn't make the team." Harper's hands trembled, still not taking her gaze from the package.

"Then what's in that?" Freddy made to take it from her hands, and she quickly snatched it back out of reach.

"Don't you dare," she glowered at him. "I'm savoring the moment."

"One man's savoring is another's torture. What's in the blooming thing?" Freddy asked the group at large.

The girl who'd delivered the package crumbled first. "It's her uniform—casual jacket, polo, Union Jack patch for her jacket and saddlecloth. The horse gets a rug." She blinked, suddenly looking at Carol. "I'm sorry, they only give them out to the riders today. The grooms' ones will be delivered in the mail."

Carol looked like she'd just won the lottery. "I don't care how I get it, as long as I get to wear them." Harper didn't think she'd ever seen her groom look as pleased as punch before.

"And when can I expect my parcel?" Freddy asked the girl.

"I'm sorry, what role do you have? I wasn't given directions for anyone else." Worried, she looked back the way she had come as if the answers lie there.

Freddy drew in an offended breath that only wealth and good breeding could manage. "I'll have you know, I'm the owner."

The girl looked relieved. "You don't get anything." She sweetly cut him down in size.

Crestfallen, Freddy looked completely stumped at her. "Nothing? At all? Not even a hat?"

"Nothing." Harper hid a grin at the brutal rebuttal.

"I wonder if maybe a car would suffice." Freddy sniffed, straightening his cuffs. Harper noticed they were etched with the Union Jack as well. *My, my. He really had committed to the team idea.*

"I don't believe there's a budget for cars." The girl now looked poised on the edge of flight.

Freddy smiled indulgently back at her. "Never mind, my dear. I'll simply purchase it for myself as a celebratory gift. After all, I'm worth it."

Harper let her smile blossom. *He's more than worth it.* Not that he needed her input at all.

HARPER STARED at the computer screen, the team photo gazing back at her. They were all there in the line-up, the riders, team vets, selectors, grooms. She was half surprised that Freddy hadn't made a last-minute bid to throw himself into the frame. Her smile slowly faded as a strange sense of unease grew the more she looked at it. It wasn't obvious straightaway, but when everyone else was in sharp focus, somehow she was blurred. The more she looked at it, the more ghostlike she appeared. Shuddering, Harper snapped her laptop shut. It was time for her to start riding horses anyway. Resolutely, she zipped up her jacket and headed out from the stable office, leaving freaky optical illusions behind her.

Several horses later, she was back to her usual determined pragmatic self, no longer jumping at shadows. "You must be Harper." Turns out a strong Russian accent was still enough to make her jerk in fright.

"Hello, Harper, I don't think you've met Dmitri before." Bella stood slightly behind her boyfriend in what looked for all the world like a submissive position.

Harper could feel her expression harden at the scenario in front of her. It was only with a supreme amount of willpower that she didn't kick him out of her stable yard right then. That and the fact she adored Bella.

"Hello." She tried her best to channel neutrality. *I am Switzerland.* She looked at Dmitri, her mouth tightening. "No, I haven't." She couldn't quite bring herself to extend her hand in greeting. She quickly glanced around, relief washing though her as she noted that, for whatever reason, Freddy had not yet taken up his customary position in the sun with his newspaper. *Small mercies.*

"Dmitri insisted on coming to see me ride this morning," Bella said brightly, clearly ignoring the strange undertones this meeting had taken on.

"And to meet the dressage rider I've heard so much about." Dmitri had a hard, cold-eyed smile that made Harper feel as warm and fuzzy as cuddling a snake. "I cannot stay long. I have other business that needs my attention. Now, Bella, do not embarrass me. Go start riding." Eyes cast downward, Bella walked with stooped shoulders toward where Carol had finished tacking her horse up. "I apologize for the time you've wasted listening to her chatter. She can be tiresome at times."

His contemptuous tone sparked her anger. "Bella is never anything but a pleasure to have around. In fact, if I'm not careful, she'll end up stealing clients from me. She has a beautiful touch with the young horses."

"I think you are being overly generous, however it keeps her amused." Dmitri made a show of looking around. "I do not see her overzealous brother about. Does he not come here every day?"

The hairs on the back of her neck stood up. Unnerved, she tried to squelch the sensation that he knew a little too much about the comings and goings of her stable yard. After all, it was plausible that Bella had simply told him about each of her days. "I expect he'll be here any minute."

Having finished her warmup, Bella pulled her mount to the arena fence closest to them. "Dmitri, isn't she just a sweetheart?"

Bored, Dmitri glanced down at his Rolex. "If you say so. Andrei will stay with you, I have business that I need to attend." He raised dead looking eyes to meet Harper's. "Bella misses her brother very much. Tomorrow night, I expect both of you for dinner. Bella will give you the details."

Not trusting herself to be civil in her reply, she simply buried her hands deeper into her pockets and walked away. What on earth was she going to tell Freddy? And more importantly, how was she going to stop him from wanting to rip Dmitri apart, when that was what she wanted to do herself?

CHAPTER 14

Freddy had grown up surrounded by wealth. The gentry didn't splash it around the way the nouveau riche did. To be fair, he liked to splash it around a little more than most of the elite, preferring to stay well away from hunting prints and chintz, but he'd never strayed into vulgarity the way Dmitri's mansion had descended.

Gold was everywhere. Not as tasteful accents, but as the main material. The banister of the sweeping stairs was gold and Freddy suspected not just gold leaf, more like solid. Every available surface was shiny and sparkly, artistic nudes gracing the walls. A modeling agency meets Ibiza with a dash of social influencer. It was enough to send his refined, albeit jaded senses into a state of protest.

"Bold interior design choices," Harper murmured. Freddy wasn't sure if it was meant as a compliment or an insult. The way Dmitri smugly looked around at his treasure, it was clear that he'd chosen to interpret it as the former.

"I like to be surrounded by the finer things in life. Art, culture, a girlfriend with a title." There was a crude undertone to his words as he dismissed Bella as simply another possession. Bella's gaze was downcast, and it was impossible to tell what she thought of the comment as she stood to one side.

"It has always been true, that old saying. What was it again?" Freddy snapped his fingers as if trying to remember. "Money can't buy taste."

"I think you'll find that if you have enough money, you don't care." Dmitri sneered.

"Clearly, old chap, you do. Everything about this house screams that you want people to notice you. Did Mother dear not love you enough growing up?" He grinned evilly at the Russian. "Did you wet the bed a lot? It can be quite traumatic on a child's psyche."

Dmitri appeared to be chewing glass from the daggers he cast Freddy's way. Harper smoothly stepped between the two of them, taking Bella's hands in her own. "I love your dress." She glanced down at her own. "It's a rare treat to be able to put a frock on for once. I swear I spend all my time in trousers."

Bella brightened under her friend's warm compliment. "Thank you. It's new."

"I do not like her wearing anything that is from last season, it's so common." Dmitri inserted himself back into the conversation.

Freddy hated the way Bella seemed to crumble in on herself. Blood began to pound at his temples, and then Harper's hand, cool and soothing against the heat of his anger, melted it away enough that he could harness it. "I think you'll find that Mother didn't raise any of her children to be common. In fact, Bella has some of the finest education money can buy. Personally, I always envisaged her as a foreign diplomat or working for the UN. I guess I got the foreign part of it right at least."

"She has proven to be quite adept at keeping foreign relationships … pleasant." *I'm going to wipe that smirk right off his face.* Freddy took a step forward, restrained by the lightest of pressures from Harper's hand. Dmitri's gaze dropped to where it rested. "I see she controls you as easily as she does that stallion she rides." Innuendo laced every word.

"I think you'll find that I have a relationship with each of them based on respect. Something that, the more time I spend with you, I realize is an alien concept for you." Freddy didn't think he'd ever been prouder of Harper, and he'd been proud of her many times since he'd become Denny's owner.

"Do you think this relationship of mutual respect will allow you to win the European Championships?" The Russian toyed with his glass, raising dead eyes to look at her speculatively.

There was something unsettling in his gaze that made Freddy step between the two of them. "She has as much chance as anyone. Probably more."

"How much more?" *Why was he so interested?*

A servant came and whispered to Bella. "Dinner," she announced, turning toward the others, cutting through the tension.

"I think you will find that my chef is incomparable." Dmitri linked arms with Bella and escorted her into the room, clearly expecting the others to follow.

"He would have to be to give me my appetite back after having been in the same room as that insufferable jerk," Freddy whispered to Harper. "How about we just turn around and leave? I think we have a few minutes before his ego notices."

Harper giggled and tapped his arm lightly, his tensed muscles relaxing under her touch. "But Bella would, and she's why we're here."

Freddy heaved a sigh, allowing her to set the pace. "Things we do for family." *And love.*

THE LIGHTS from the passing cars reflected off Freddy's face. For all the warmth there, it might as well be etched from granite. Pensively, Harper gazed at him, wishing she could bring back the jester that had always resided so close to the surface. The more she'd got to know him, the more she'd realized that it was his defense that he hid behind. To now see him stripped of it, it scared her.

"I understand why you want Bella away from him so badly. There's something so cold about him, and the way he treats her like a possession is awful." She shuddered at the dead look Bella had worn for the dinner, like anything would set him off. When she'd had a chance to speak to her privately when she'd been shown the bathroom, Harper had noticed a bruise hidden behind a wide cuff bracelet and makeup. She'd wanted to bundle her from the mansion that very instant but knew that Bella wasn't ready to leave. Not yet.

Freddy's knuckles cracked as he tightened his grip on the steering wheel. "When you figure out a way, let me know. I've been jolly well trying ever since they got together and I'm still no closer to making it happen. Maybe I should just kidnap her until she comes to her senses."

"Is it wrong that I think that might not be a bad idea?" Freddy's car pulled to a halt in front of her stable yard. Her little two-room apartment tucked away in the corner. "Freddy?"

He turned tormented eyes to her. "What do I do, Harper?"

"What you're doing. Make sure she knows that you love her and we're here for her. She's a smart girl, she'll figure it out." *I hope.* The words clearly not erasing the pain in his soul, she did the only thing she knew to do. She pulled him close until she felt his uneven breathing on her cheek and tried to kiss the worry from his eyes, if only for a moment.

CHAPTER 15

When Harper was little, she'd lay in her bed under the cover her mother had made by stitching together her precious horse prize ribbons and stare at the posters on her wall, pretending she was one of them. When most girls her age had had pop stars, she'd had horse riders, and her favorite ones had always been the dressage riders. Late into the night, she'd pretend that she was on the team with them, riding for the gold medal. In those days, with her childish innocence, she'd believed anything was possible.

A lot of years later combined with blood, sweat and tears, not to mention a complete lack of social life, and she'd come as close as she'd ever come. The European Championships. Standing with the team, she knew that somewhere in the crowd—most likely in a VIP suite—was Freddy. The opening ceremony drew her in. Whimsical in its fairytale elements, drawing on the rich cultural heritage of the host nation of Sweden, Harper felt her emotions well up. *She was here. Little Harper Ferguson was actually standing here with a Union Jack on her blazer, watching the opening ceremony for the European Championships.*

"A little over-the-top if you ask me." Caroline Fitzsimmon, her teammate, sniffed.

Clearly, at her sixth straight championship and having been selected for two Olympics, the thrill of opening ceremonies had well and truly become tarnished. Harper thought it would never lose its luster, no matter how many she attended. At least, she hoped this wasn't her only one.

"I thought all the blonde girls added a little something to it," William Smitherson the final team member added with a leer. He had quite the reputation for all his stable girls being fair, leggy, and not over the age of twenty-four. Harper shivered. It would have been so easy to end up in a stable like that when she'd been young and with stars in her eyes. In fact, she'd had his poster on her wall. Instead, she'd ridden horses that no one else had wanted to touch—the talented but crazy horses—and with each success, a few better horses had come her way until she'd finally been able to open her own yard.

And then Denny had come her way … and with him, Freddy. It was funny how it had all worked out. The horse of a lifetime had brought her the love of a lifetime. A flutter of nerves stirred at the thought. *Love.* It was true. She was head over heels in love with Freddy, and she knew he cared about her. Heck, he had involved himself in every aspect of her life. And not in a controlling, intimidating way—the Russian sprung to mind—but rather with an infectious enthusiasm that sparkled with pride of her. And yet, they'd never talked about the future away from horses. He was titled, and she remembered his parents being quite the snobs back in the day about those who weren't. And she wasn't.

She followed her teammates out of the main arena, her thoughts still on Freddy. Bella was with the Russian, and he had no title. But then again, he was a billionaire and maybe that made up for the lack of title and the fact he was mafia. Freddy didn't really talk about his parents. Maybe they didn't have much influence over his choice of life partner. Harper pulled her mind away from that line of thought. He hadn't even said he loved her, let alone talked about marriage. Not really. Why was she even thinking about it at a time like this? A couple of minutes earlier, she'd been on the verge of emotional tears—the ugly kind, too—and now she was thinking about marrying Freddy? *Girl, this is not the way to handle pre-competition nerves.*

Giving herself a mental shake, she peeled away from the others and headed to where Denny was stabled. Carol was helping the bay stallion settle in, but given the state Harper found herself in, she just hoped her horse hadn't fallen madly in love with the equine stabled beside him. That was the last thing she needed.

FREDDY HADN'T BEEN EXPECTING Cirque du Soleil to meet the Brothers Grimm for the opening ceremony entertainment, but it had worked. A thrill had coursed through him. He wasn't here as a spectator at some sort of fancy event. He was here as part of a team. Maybe not directly as part of the United Kingdom Team, but of one better. Team Harper. He still wasn't sure what he'd ever done in life to deserve a spot on that particular team, and if he was honest, he probably didn't. But he was going to grab hold of this with everything he had and never let it go. *Never let love go.*

Love. What a frivolous emotion. For sure, he and Bella had been raised without it and he was certain his mother and father hadn't felt the need to have it when they'd married, a socially advantageous and suitable spouse of greater importance. Clearly that hadn't been important to his friends, each having married solely for love and to amazing women. *The lucky sods.*

Freddy clapped politely as the Championships was officially opened, nodding to various other owners and sponsors —some he was on rather familiar grounds with now that he was a regular fixture on the dressage competition scene—as he rose to his feet. In a complex this large, he knew with complete certainty where he'd find Harper. *The stables.*

Whistling happily to himself, he made his way through the mass of humanity. A hard knock almost sent him flying. Prepared to give umbrage to the insolent who had run into him, Freddy turned, fists balled. The Russian smirked at him with, to Freddy's surprise, Silvio beside him. Raising a brow that only centuries of superior breeding could instill, he stared them both down. *How did they even know each other?*

"Did you come to see what the horse you lost is doing?"

"My wife still hasn't forgiven me." Silvio sucked his thick lips. "It's a good thing my mistress still loves me."

"I'm not sure Svetlana is the loving kind." Dmitri gave him a thin-lipped sneer. "At least not when I knew her."

Uneasiness whispered through Freddy. Dmitri was like a disease, spreading his tentacles over everyone and everything, waiting for the opportune time to wring out every last droplet of value with a snap of his fingers. "It makes sense. You're not exactly the warm and fuzzy teddy bear sort of chap, are you?" Freddy retorted in cold sarcasm.

"That's a bit rough." Silvio jerked a glance up to the Russian like a cowed hound dog fearful of his master.

"Your sister has no complaints. At least none that she would dare utter aloud." Dmitri's eyes narrowed, filling with cold malice.

Freddy clenched his hands, still in fists. "How about I

make some complaints on her behalf? It might be a little different coming from someone who isn't afraid of you."

"They might not start off afraid, but believe me, everyone always learns by the end. I'm what you would call an expert at getting that reaction." Freddy shuddered inwardly at the implications in the other man's ominous words.

"How about everyone calms down." Silvio glanced uneasily around. *Maybe he was worried his wife would come and drag him away.* "Did either of you know you can bet on the outcome here? Adds a little more spice to it."

"I haven't gambled in months." Freddy forced his cramped lungs to exhale. *Do not let the Russian drag you down to his level. You're better than this.*

"Such a shame. Look what it's given you. A shiny horse, a lovely young woman." Dmitri's mouth took an unpleasant twist. "Horse riding is a dangerous sport. It would be a shame if she got hurt. Do you ever worry about that?"

His voice was completely emotionless, and it chilled Freddy to his core. "I don't worry about her with the horses."

"That is good that you trust in her safety. It plays on a man's mind. Worry about his loved ones, it is a burden." Dmitri's gaze bored into Freddy's like a dentist drill.

"I assume someone told you that. I highly doubt you've ever been plagued by such emotions." Freddy's muscles tightened, ready for battle.

Dmitri laughed joylessly. "Bella is always telling me how funny you are. She's right, you're quite the clown." He looked at his lackey. "I think we have left the ladies to their own devices for long enough." He returned his frigid gaze to Freddy. "Bella is quite keen to catch up. Harper is, after all, the reason we're here."

"Bella is welcome anytime." The narrowing of the other man's eyes let Freddy know that the slight hadn't been missed. "Now, if you'll excuse me, I'm jolly well done with this conversation." With long purposeful strides as if he could expend the negative energy that swirled within him, Freddy left, not halting in his progress until he had gathered Harper close and kissed her desperately.

"What was that for?" Harper clutched at her chest breathlessly, smiling up at him.

"Aren't I allowed to kiss a beautiful woman?" The words glibly spilled from his lips, hopefully hiding the dark shadows that tormented him.

Possessively, she pulled his face closer to hers. "As long as it's only me."

His heart beat faster. His woman doesn't share. Something primal roared to life in him at odds with his character. The force of the emotion pushed his uneasiness from the earlier exchange down deeper. *His woman.* He wasn't sure what the Russian was up to, but he wasn't going to allow anything to happen to her. Not while he drew breath.

CHAPTER 16

*G*limpses of her surrounds broke through the wall of concentration she'd built around herself to keep her nerves at bay as Harper warmed up her horse. A fellow competitor to one side, a coach yelling out last minute instructions, a horse whinnying in the distance. Somehow the steady rhythm of Denny's hoofbeats and his proud, gleaming neck in front of her kept her grounded. She breathed, trying to keep her pulse from racing. *We've competed against all of these people before and beaten a great many of them.*

A vise tightened over her chest. Last night, Freddy had been oddly needy and yet far away at the same time, and today, it was like she'd forgotten to ride. The expectations resting on her choked her confidence away. This was not how she'd expected to feel at her first Championships. Harper swallowed hard, biting back the tears that threatened. Setting her jaw, she straightened in the saddle. *Toughen up, Buttercup. If I didn't cry when Freddy dumped me in the manure heap, I sure as heck am not going to do it now.* Shifting her weight, she put her leg on, signaling Denny to half-pass. *I'm here to win.* Pushing all her doubts away, she moved as one with her horse. *And I can't do it sniffling in the corner.*

～

I LET HER DOWN. The thought haunted Freddy as he sat in his privileged surroundings. Harper had needed him to be present, and instead he'd merely been able to go through the barest of motions before finding himself clinging to her as a child would for comfort. It hadn't been fair to her. This time —this championship—was about her. Her chance to shine. And yet now he was scared that he'd tarnish it.

He signaled the attendant to refill his glass. It had never failed to stop him from caring—at least too much—before.

"Isn't it a little early?" Bella asked, settling herself down. Even inside, she'd hidden her features behind oversized sunglasses, her hair pulled to frame her face—*or hide it.*

Freddy glanced behind her, surprised when he only spied Andrei. "Is it too much to hope the Russian has died or in the very least departed from the country?" The attendant silently went about his task. "And if that's the case, then it's never too early for a celebration." He quirked a brow at her. "Care to join me?"

"When in Rome, or in this case, Sweden." Bella shrugged. "And Dmitri is simply on a business call and will be joining us shortly."

Freddy nodded the attendant toward his sister, his own wineglass hovering inches from his lips. The siren call of the numbing liquid promised, with a knowledge that came from long familiarity, to absolve him of all his worries as long as he consumed enough for his capacity to care to be void. But did he really want that? Resolutely, he drained it, gesturing for another top-up.

"Pity. I quite enjoy the idea of you as a widow. Black has always been your color."

"I look good in any color," Bella tartly retorted. It was good to see a glimpse of his spirited sister—the one he used to know. She took a sip of her own wine. "But black has always been good to me."

"Have I ever told you how modest you are?"

"It's not immodesty if it's the truth."

"Touché."

"Now, tell me, how was Harper feeling this morning? Is she handling the nerves?" Bella looked out toward the main arena as though she would find the answer somewhere in the grains of sand.

"Yes, Freddy, how is Harper feeling?" The wine soured in Freddy's mouth at the Russian's interruption. *Was it too much to ask that his business calls keep him tied up all morning?* Anger coiled tightly in his stomach as he watched the impact of Dmitri's arrival on Bella, the animation from only moments earlier was lost as her expression became shuttered.

"Harper is a complete professional, and any nerves she's experiencing, I am sure she will harness to her advantage." Freddy's casual tone belied the fire in his eyes.

"Excellent. It would be a shame if she failed to rise to the occasion given all the hype around her." Dmitri inspected his perfectly manicured nails. "I believe there is quite a bit of interest surrounding her."

"I don't think there is anything to worry about. When I spoke to Harper, she was incredibly focused," Bella chimed in support of her friend, quickly sinking into herself when Dmitri fixed his attention on her.

"Did I ask your opinion?"

"No," she replied in a small voice, her eyes sliding away toward the tablecloth.

"Then keep quiet." Dmitri coldly stared at his girlfriend.

Was it possible to have hatred burn ice cold rather than hot? Freddy set his glass carefully on the table. After all, it didn't deserve to be caught up as collateral damage. "I'd watch your tone when you talk to my sister, old chap."

"I think you'll find that your sister doesn't appreciate your interference." Dmitri snapped his fingers at Bella. Freddy watched in disbelief as she stood woodenly. "Go get me some canapés."

"That's what the attendant is for," Freddy said. "Bella, sit down."

"Freddy, I don't mind. Is there anything in particular you want?" Bella asked, looking blankly at her boyfriend.

"I'll leave it up to your discretion, but if I find a trace of coriander, you know what the punishment is." Dmitri, threat finished, settled himself back into his seat.

Freddy could only watch in disbelief as his sister slung away. Ah, there it was. The ice-cold hatred twisting itself around until the scalding burn flowed like lava through his veins. "Get away from me, and while you're at it, stay away from my sister!"

Dmitri idly swirled his glass. "Why would I want to do that?"

"Because it would be best for your health."

"I think you have only a faint grasp on what would be good for either your sister's or your health." The Russian stopped his incessant swirling. "Did you know, they have shortened the odds on Harper winning. But losing, now that is where it gets interesting. Say if she was to fail in the freestyle, some sort of misstep, it might prove to be quite rewarding."

Disgusted, Freddy could only stare at the other man. Was he suggesting what he thought he was? "I'm not sure I follow."

"I think you are not as stupid as you pretend. It would be mutually beneficial if your girlfriend wasn't to win."

Freddy pounded his fist on the table. "There's no way I'm asking her to throw this competition," he snarled. "You want me to ask her to throw away what she's spent years dreaming and training for? Clearly you're delusional."

Those cold eyes fastened on him, sucking the warmth from the air around them. "Because I have your sister. You always want to stick your nose in my business, running your mouth about me, so now I make you my business. I have a lot of money tied up in the outcome of this competition and I would be very upset if I lost it because you can't control your girlfriend. Or is it some sort of ill-conceived noble impulse you've discovered?" Dmitri tut-tutted mockingly. "It's sweet, but not incredibly practical." He drained his glass, setting it back on the table. Freddy could only watch sullenly. "I would hate for my discontent to spill over onto your sister or perhaps your girlfriend." Dmitri stood, toying with the ornate ring on his pinky finger. "Think about it, but be quick. I only have so much patience for disobedience." Satisfied his warning had been received, he gave him a last smirk before departing.

The urge to pick up the floral centerpiece from the table and hurl it at the back of the jerk's head was overpowering and yet Freddy sat motionless, frozen in place as another rider entered the ring. Defeated, he knew that Dmitri had him. He would never risk his sister, nor—no matter how mad she would be—Harper.

CHAPTER 17

*A*ll too quickly, Freddy ran out of diversions and was forced, completely against his natural inclination, to confront his dilemma face on. With only three combinations to go until Harper, he knew with dreadful clarity that he was caught between the proverbial rock and a hard place. If she didn't do well here, it wasn't the end of the dream for her. There would still be other championships and, God willing, the Olympics. She may never forgive him, but at least she'd be safe and alive to be able to have the opportunity again. So would Bella. At least until he could get her head on straight and get her the heck away from Dmitri.

With a jolt, Freddy joined in with applause for the combination that had just completed their dressage test. Leaning forward, he read the names on the scoreboard and, caught off-guard, he realized that he'd lost track of two riders and Harper was about to enter the stadium.

No matter what happened after this, he knew that nothing would take away from Harper's moment in the spotlight. She deserved it, and it was the least he could do before he snatched it all away. At least for now. *Damn that Russian to*

Hell! His nails bit into the palm of his hand, the pain nothing compared to the searing regret racking his soul. *I'll make it up to you.* He swore, gazing intently at the focused young woman in the ring. *I promise.*

THE GREAT HORSE moved seamlessly through his test, each movement a testament to his power and grace and her training. Somehow it felt like she cantered up to the judges' hut to acknowledge them and then, before she knew it, she was halting on the centerline giving them a salute, and yet it all felt like slow motion at the same time. One thing Harper was completely convinced of was that she was one of the luckiest people in the world to experience it.

Patting Denny's lathered neck as she walked him back toward the stable area, she looked around, not yet ready to come down off her cloud. "My beautiful boy, I have so many carrots waiting for you," Carol crooned, walking alongside them.

"Anything he wants, he gets." Harper's cheeks hurt from the grin that seemed to have taken up residence on her face. "For the rest of his life." In the distance, security pass swinging around his neck, she could see Freddy making his way over. She slipped her feet from her stirrups and slid gracefully from the stallion. "Be good for Carol." She gave his neck another pat.

"He always is," the groom declared loyally as she gathered the reins over his head and began to lead him away.

Running awkwardly in her top boots, Harper closed the distance between them and threw herself in his arms. "Did you see us?" She giggled, her emotions running away on her. "Of course you did. I don't think Denny has done better in his whole life."

"You guys were something else out there." Freddy spoke in an odd, yet gentle tone. "I've never felt so privileged in my entire life, being part of this."

"You wait. If we keep going like this, we might very well end up with a medal." She stared off into the distance. "Imagine that. Harper Ferguson and her wonder horse, Denny, European Dressage Champions."

It was the silence that greeted her statement that sent the first sliver of ice through her. The way he couldn't meet her eyes finished it off. "I've decided to withdraw Denny from the rest of the competition."

Harper could only stare at him. "But why? I don't understand. He's completely sound, and I'm currently at the top of the leaderboard," she said in a choked voice.

"As his owner, I've had to make the decision that is right." Freddy's words barely registered among the dizzying vortex of emotions she now found herself in.

"Then make the right one." She stumbled, trying to articulate her shocked thoughts. "I don't know where this has come from, but change it."

"I'm doing it, and its final." He chewed off the words, as if stopping more from slipping out.

"How could I be such an idiot?" she cried, forcing the lump in her throat down. "I thought you cared. But you don't care about anything. You never have. But I do care. About this horse, about this championship, about my dreams." With each word, she jabbed viciously at his chest, trying to hurt him the same way he was hurting her.

He slowly raised his eyes to meet hers. "You're wrong. I do care," he said, broken.

"Maybe about your sister. Then go away and care about her, but leave me the heck alone and let me do what I came here to do. Win."

"I care about you a great deal more than I think you realize, Harper." Anguish swam in his eyes.

Suffocating betrayal threatened to smother her. "Why are you being so cruel?"

Freddy shook his head slowly. "I always wanted to make people laugh. I thought that was the most important thing in the world, to be liked." He swallowed. "But it turns out that it's protecting the ones you love. If you must hate me, then I'll live with that. If you never speak to me again, my heart will stop beating. But it won't change my mind." He reached out a hand to stroke her cheek. Furious, she jerked out of reach. Sad, he turned and walked away, taking Harper's shattered dreams with him.

FREDDY DIDN'T KNOW if he'd ever get over the sight of Harper's expression turning from jubilation to her dream lying in carnage around her. She was a woman who held a grudge, and there was every likelihood that he had forced her from his life forever. His misery began so acutely it pained him to breathe.

"Nicely done," a Texan twang said, a figure emerging from the shadows.

Freddy's mind skittered about like a fresh colt, the torment of heartbreak taking pause as he stared at the other man as if he was a Pit Bull speaking Cantonese. Uncomfortable, he was aware that the silence had stretched out, all while his mouth was open like a drowning fish.

"It's not good form to snoop on one's betters, Andrei—or is it now Andy or Chip?"

A smile stretched his normally dour looking lips, looking out of place. "I think it's best for everyone that you still know me as Andrei."

"Okay, Andrei, what does Dmitri want now?" Freddy was at rock bottom. He failed to think there was anything the Russian could add that would make things worse.

"I'm sure Dmitri has all sorts of plans for you and your sister, but that's not why I'm here. But I'm sure it will provide the motivation for you to provide your assistance."

Freddy rubbed at the bridge of his nose. "Look, old chap, I'm not really in the mood to complete a cryptic crossword. So if you could just jolly well come and say whatever it is, then I can be on my merry way to somewhere with liquor and cards."

"Alcohol in the quantities that you drink it isn't good for your cognitive reasoning." Andrei looked him over appraisingly. "I thought you'd slowed down in the last several months."

"Let's just say I had another diversion and now that's over." The other man's words penetrated the miasma of his brain. "How do you know what I have and have not been drinking?"

"It's my job." He pulled out a badge, flicking it open. "FBI."

A great gust of hysterical laughter erupted from Freddy, and he made a show of looking around. "Very funny. Was Stirling in on this?" He leaned in closer. "Look, I'm not sure how much he's paying you, but if Dmitri finds out you're just an actor, you're going to end up swimming with the fishes."

"Trust me, I know exactly what I'm involved with, and it's outside of your producer friend's imagination. I've been working on the inside for quite some time, and it's come to our attention, given your desire to extract your sister from her current predicament, that you might be inclined to be of assistance."

"I give. What assistance?" He had to give it to the other man, he had complete commitment to the role. Freddy made a mental note to commend him to Stirling when he next spoke to him. The man was a natural.

"We have quite a bit of evidence on Dmitri with someone helping from the inside. We want you to wear a wire to record your conversations with him. We understand that he wants you to get your rider to throw the event."

"He does, but if you really work for who you say you do, why would him wanting to rig the results of a dressage championship be of the least concern? Don't you have bigger fish to fry?"

"We are building a case against him, but it's not enough to hold him yet. But this is enough to get him off the streets where he can't hurt any more people." Zealous fire shone from Andrei's eyes.

"Speaking of more people getting hurt, what about Bella and Harper?"

"I can personally guarantee that they will be provided discreet protection. If we play this right, they won't even know what's happening."

Freddy caught himself glancing uneasily over his shoulder, expecting boogeymen to jump from the shadows. "And if I agree, that's it? Just wear a wire?"

"We will want you to pretend to go along with Dmitri's plan, however, have your rider compete. It will flush out Dmitri when he doesn't get what he wants."

A quick and disturbing thought struck at Freddy. He was damned either way. "And you promise nothing will happen to Bella or Harper?'

"We will do everything in our power to keep everyone safe, including you."

"I'm glad I'm jolly included in that scenario, but given an option, I want their safety to be valued over my own." He sighed. *If ever there was a time to get rotten drunk.* "I'll do it."

Andrei gripped his hand in a firm clasp. "There are a lot of people who will be avenged by this."

"Honestly, I don't care about anything except getting my sister away and keeping the woman I love safe. Anything else doesn't factor in for me." Freddy knew it was selfish, but those two women were his sole motivation.

The spy gave a sharp nod of understanding before melting back into the shadows, leaving Freddy with the unsettling predicament of wondering if he'd imagined the whole thing.

CHAPTER 18

The agony of heartbreak twisted with the painful disillusionment of lost dreams as Harper helped Carol load their gear into the horse lorry. "I don't understand. I though he wanted this as much as us," muttered the groom.

You and me both. It hurt how little she actually knew him. *He must be laughing with his friends about gullible little Harper Ferguson—"I tricked her again." And his sister! Was she in on it, too?*

"Can I have a moment?" Freddy's face peered into the lorry. If she didn't know better, she'd have thought he seemed anxious, or at the very least, stressed. *Well, let him be after how he's treated us.*

"I can give you both a moment." Carol looked quickly at Harper as if to gauge if that was the right move.

"You might want to hear what I have to say." He looked over his shoulder slightly. "At least the first part."

Carol widened her eyes, silently asking what to do. Harper put her out of her misery with a quick nod. "Whatever you have to say, make it quick. We have to finish load-ing." Her voice was hoarse with frustration.

Freddy fumbled with his pocket, pulling out a flask, and with shaky hands, unscrewed it, gulping it down. *Typical. He acts like a jerk and then drinks to numb the consequences.* Harper glared at him with burning, reproachful eyes. Swallowing hard, he gathered himself. "I've changed my mind."

"About what, exactly?" Her fury almost choked her, her hurt fighting to finish the job. "About drinking? About us? Tell me, Freddy, what is it that's made you come down here and grace us with your presence?"

He winced. "I deserve that."

"No, actually you deserve a lot more than that. But I'm a professional and I won't give everyone here anymore cause for speculation than they already have."

"I'm sorry, Harper. I thought I was doing the right thing. But I see now that it wasn't. You and Denny are still in the competition." He looked at her for all the world like he expected her to jump into his arms and smother his face with kisses.

Harper's anger became a scalding fury. "Excuse me? Now you've decided? What happens if I don't want to anymore?" she spat contemptuously.

"Harper, don't be silly. You and I both jolly well know how much you want this."

It was then that she experienced something she never had. She actually became speechless with unbridled rage. "Silly? You're calling me silly," she screeched.

"Easy, Harper," Carol soothed, looking like she wanted to be anywhere but there.

"See, even Carol thinks you're overreacting." Freddy smiled gratefully at the groom.

"Oh, don't even go there. I said it because I agree that Harper doesn't need to give anyone more fodder for gossip."

Carol put her hands on her hips. "And I don't understand how you're not ashamed of yourself, putting Harper through this."

"You have no idea how much I don't want to be doing any of this," he said in a broken voice. Harper's heart lurched. *Don't be silly,* she scalded herself. *He brought this on himself.*

"You're sabotaging me, and I don't understand why. I thought we had something special. Was this all some sort of elaborate scheme? I'm such an idiot for falling for your lies." Her chest constricted, forcing the air from her lungs.

"I think you should leave now," Carol said sternly. "You've delivered your news, and now Harper needs time to refocus. She hasn't performed the new freestyle at a competition before and that's stressing her enough without you adding to her load."

Harper closed her eyes. She just wanted to pretend that none of this was happening. She heard Carol's sharp intake of breath and then felt a tender touch on her cheek. "I need you to trust me, Harper."

Bitterness at his sheer arrogance streaked rancid through her. She shoved his hand away. "I don't believe anything that comes out of your mouth at this point."

His eyes begged her. *To what? Forgive him? Understand?* "If you only believe one thing I say, I want you to believe this. I know this doesn't make any sense right now, but I love you and I want you to go out there and kick butt." He looked like he wanted to reach out to her again—to kiss her. Harper trembled in torment. "Everything else, we can sort out afterwards."

As if sensing that he'd gone as far as he could, he gave her one last beseeching look before turning and, with shoulders stooped, walked dejectedly away. Harper's face crumbled, and with a sob, she hurried to the front of the lorry to muffle her tears. She wasn't going to give anyone the satisfaction of seeing her cry over a broken heart.

~

DEVASTATION so pure it robbed him of any coherent thought assailed Freddy. How had he gotten to his point so quickly? Coming to the Championships had been fueled by dreams and passion. Seeing Harper so close to achieving her next goal, it had seemed like, as a couple, anything was possible. Goodness, he'd even considered what the next step might be for them. Something revolving around breakfasts together in the mornings and meeting her parents. And like a cloud of smoke, it was gone.

With a shaking hand, he fished around in his pocket to retrieve his flask, draining the last droplets from it. Frustrated, he threw it away from him. "Temper, temper. Cool heads are what are needed in this type of situation."

Freddy glowered at the Russian-slash-Texan. Nothing would delight him more than knocking him on his behind. "I wouldn't be in this if it wasn't for you."

"Actually, I'm your chance at salvation. You're in this predicament because your sister made some poor life choices, and you couldn't leave it alone." The truth drove a spike into the eviscerated remains of his heart. "Now then." Andrei rubbed his hands together matter-of-factly. "There are a few things I need to brief you on."

"Great." Freddy couldn't even muster the enthusiasm to make it sound authentic.

"Tomorrow morning, a chap called Pietro will bring you your breakfast at the hotel. While there, you will be wired up. Any conversation you have with Dmitri from that point forth will be recorded. I need you to act natural, but keep the conversations flowing. You won't see them, but there will be agents around you, your sister and Harper at all times." Andrei peered closer at the sullen man. "Chin up, son, it'll be over soon enough."

Freddy gave him a humorless smile. The man spoke more truth than he might know. "I think it already is."

Andrei gave him a strange look, as if questioning his suitability for the task assigned him. The joke's on him. Turns out that he was never suitable, especially now that he tried to accept that Harper may never forgive him.

he red-headed Pietro proved to not be the most noteworthy thing of Freddy's strange morning. It was mind-boggling given the copious amounts of alcohol he'd self-medicated with the previous evening that he was even capable of noting anything.

"Thank you for shaving, it makes my job a lot easier."

Freddy flinched as Pietro's cold hand made contact with his chest. "Thanks, but I didn't do it especially for this. Good grooming makes a man, after all."

"Regardless, it still makes things easier," Pietro brushed his correction aside and set about his task. "Once I've finished wiring you up, just act natural, speak as you usually would. Don't try to project your voice or speak louder, our equipment is able to pick up most things."

"Got it. Act natural, don't overact."

The agent laughed. "That's a good one. Mind if I borrow it?"

"Completely fine, old chap." *Completely fine.* What a strange concept. He hadn't seen Harper since the day before when she'd come to collect her things from the guest bedroom in the hotel suite and informed him that, since their relationship was strictly professional, she'd return to staying in the horse lorry. *Yes, everything was completely fine.*

"You're all done. Do you have any questions?"

Will you convince my girlfriend to forgive me? "None."

"Excellent. Good luck. I hope we get something today." Putting his little box of equipment back in the secret compartment of his trolley, Pietro seamlessly transformed from agent back to hotel busboy. With a final tweak of his uniform, he opened the door and disappeared down the hall.

Freddy gave his chest a cautious scratch, careful not to dislodge any of Pietro's hard work. Finding himself at loose ends, he made a decision. Draining the last of his tea, he snatched a jacket off the back of a chair and followed in the agent's tracks. If this was going to be his last day, he wasn't going to spend it cooped up in here.

MAYBE HE SHOULD HAVE STAYED at the hotel and gone to the bar instead. Denny eyed him disdainfully, not even bothering to sniff the apple Freddy held out in apology. "Come on, old son, I snagged it fresh from the fruit basket this morning." He gave it an appealing waggle. "I know you like apples."

"He prefers carrots." Carol sniffed. "And I need to start getting him ready for Harper to warmup." She shouldered past him, her elbows none too gentle as she went by.

"Ouch!" Freddy grabbed at a foot she'd managed to stand on.

"Oh, are you still standing there?" She snapped the stable door firmly shut between them. "I assumed you'd gone somewhere you were wanted."

Freddy flinched at the chill in her voice. "Wish Harper luck, and I'll be cheering from the VIP box."

"Harper doesn't need luck. She has talent and determination, and I frankly don't think she'd give a fig about you cheering for her or not." Satisfied, she turned her back on him and fastened the halter on Denny, effectively dismissing Freddy.

Hoping he didn't look like a dog slinking off with his tail between his legs, which was how he felt, Freddy went in search of the comforts of the VIP box, namely the alcohol.

By his third glass, although not as comfortably numb as he would like, the sting had certainly been soothed as he gazed out over the arena. Today, on that sand, Harper would either be one step closer to her dreams or she would stumble. All Freddy had wanted to do was help her reach for the stars. Instead he'd only crushed everything she'd worked for.

"It is a marvelous morning, is it not?" Dmitri looked disgustingly refreshed. Bella silently trailed him and gave her brother a tight smile. They both knew what was at stake. Andrei took up his customary position at the entrance.

"If you say so." Freddy signaled the attendant. "Could I please have another two, no, three bottles of champagne?"

"An excellent idea," enthused Dmitri. "There will be much we will want to celebrate before the morning is over."

"I hope so," muttered Freddy, staring back toward the arena, the scoreboard in the distance.

"It was quite the nice touch to not withdraw your horse. Much more believable for her freestyle to crumble under the pressure. You must have her better trained than I had given you credit for." Dmitri smirked toward Bella. "Maybe I will share some of my training tips with you."

Freddy clenched his teeth tightly over the venom that flowed through his veins. *Soon.* His hand casually rubbed at the front of shirt, straightening the fabric over the microphone concealed beneath. *Soon.*

THE WOMAN STARING BACK at her in the mirror was glassy-eyed as she secured her pin to her stock. The diamonds sparkled with a glee that was at odds with Harper's own emotions. Her hands stilled, toying with the edges of the jewelry. She still had her plain, old one somewhere, She still had time to replace this one. Harper traced the filigree. She hadn't worn the other one for a while. It was bound to be tarnished, the gloss having worn off. But wasn't that quite the metaphor for her own life. Groaning, she rested her head in her hands. She was so tired of feeling miserable and confused. Straightening, she stared herself straight in the eye.

"Harper Ferguson, you are a winner. Get your mind in the game and there is no stopping you." She swallowed over the swell of emotions that choked her last words. "You are enough. You only need Denny to make your dreams come true." Picking up her white gloves from the counter in front of her, she gave herself one final once-over. *If only she believed her own words.*

THE MAHOGANY BAY stallion's coat gleamed, the light reflecting as the muscles beneath rippled as they contracted and released. On his back, his rider sat poised, waiting for the first strains of her music to begin. Freddy didn't think it was possible to be any prouder of Harper than in that moment, and then the image on the big screen zoomed in and he saw the diamond brooch at her throat. It was like he was sitting in a vacuum, everything around him sucked away. The sly digs of Dmitri, the chatter and murmurings of the crowd, the smell of the platter that had been set at their table.

Nothing mattered in that moment than the horse and rider in the center of the stadium.

"They will not see it coming," Dmitri gave him a nudge in the ribs. "You are very clever with how you are executing our little plan. I, myself, have quite the experience with executions, but of a somewhat different nature." He laughed at his own joke.

Freddy smiled weakly, glancing over at Andrei. "I have the upmost confidence that everything will go to plan."

The music began as a gentle ripple of notes, a melody that haunted and cajoled the ears as Harper and Denny danced down the centerline, halting in front of the judges. The music paused as gentle as a sigh before the same melody resumed. This time a commanding beat began to drive a sense of urgency, causing the audience to collectively lean forward, anticipation building as the pair skipped joyously across the sand, each movement flawless. Pride sang sweetly through Freddy's body. The pair out there, they were his, and he was theirs. And nothing would ever stop that.

Dmitri, brows furrowed, turned to Freddy. "The mistakes, they are happening soon? You are not leaving much time."

"I think you will find that Harper has timed everything perfectly," Bella murmured. Freddy grinned at the voice of the sister he'd missed for so long.

A dark foreboding expression descended over the Russian's features as Denny thundered up the centerline and, with imperceivable commands from his slight rider, came to a perfectly square halt. Harper completed her test with a crisp salute before ecstatically patting her horse's neck.

"What have you done?" Dmitri spat out. "You are a fool. I am not the person one wants to cross."

"Oh really? Well, dear boy, it appears I have." Freddy was pretty sure that if looks could kill, Dmitri would have followed through with his unspoken threats on the spot.

"You think you're funny? Well, clown, we're going to have a little chat. Somewhere private. And I'm going to make sure that, when I'm finished with you, you'll always have a smile. One I will carve into your face."

"Dmitri, please calm down. I'm sure Freddy has a perfectly reasonable explanation. After all, he wasn't riding the horse." Bella placed a calming hand on her boyfriend's arm.

"If I wanted your input, I'd have asked for it." Dmitri sneered, knocking Bella's hand away. He turned cold eyes that burned like dry ice toward Freddy. "So, tell me, Clown, what could you say that will change this? Did you not understand? Was it difficult for you to grasp what I wanted?" Spittle flew from the enraged man's mouth. "She had to lose. Is that hard to understand?"

"Not in the least. But I decided that I didn't want Harper to throw her dreams away because some Russian jerk said so." Freddy drained his glass. "Just so we're clear, you're the Russian jerk."

With a snarl, Dmitri lunged forward, knocking the table over as he grappled to get a hold of Freddy. Bella went flying as his shoulder connected with her, landing heavily on the ground. Freddy, having never been the confrontational type, realized that he was about to be involved in his first ever physical altercation as an adult. The best he could hope for was that Andrei would put a stop to it before Dmitri broke his face.

Somehow, in the melee of Bella's screaming and the pounding of flesh against flesh, there were people pulling them apart, a furious Dmitri screaming threats in Russian. At least, that's what it sounded like. Russian was a tricky language like that. For all he knew, he was saying he loved him. He was still screaming as he was being led away.

Exhausted, Freddy picked up an overturned chair and sat

down, trying to ignore the agog crowd. *I guess it's not every day you come to a perfectly civilized dressage championship to be entertained by a screaming Russian in a fist fight in the VIP section.* He wondered if word had gotten back to Harper yet. *She'd be mortified.*

"Here." Bella held out some ice. "You'd better put this on, it's not going to stop you looking horrific, but every little thing will help, I guess." She gave a shrug. "At least you weren't that good-looking to begin with."

Freddy gave a bark of laughter. "Thanks." He looked closer at her. She was pale, her agitated eyes flicking about constantly, as if scanning for danger. *How long had she been on high alert and he hadn't even known?* "Are you all right?"

Sad eyes settled on his as she nodded. "I'm going to be all right." She picked up a napkin that had stubbornly clung to the table even as it had been flung on its side and gently dabbed at his lip. "Thank you for caring, but you need to go tell Harper about everything." His sister pressed the napkin into his hand.

Freddy stared down at the bright scarlet marring the pale fabric. "And do what? She doesn't want to talk to me. Do I go and beg for her forgiveness?" Would she even offer it to him?

Bella sunk down until she was eye level with him. "I know I'm not exactly in the position to be giving out relationship advice, but I love you, and you can't just pretend that you'll be okay if you lose Harper. You need to fight for her. She's smart and she loves you. I promise she'll understand."

Andrei appeared beside Bella. "It's time to go." It sounded strange hearing the Texan twang from the supposed Russian.

Confused, he looked between them. "Go where?"

"She didn't tell you?" Andrei looked at Bella with mild disapproval. "You should have told him."

"Told me what?" Freddy had thought all the games were over.

Bella clasped his hands, giving him a small smile. "Since I was the informant on the inside, I'm a witness. They need to put me into a protective witness program. I believe I even get a new identity. At least for a while." Her chin quivered despite her brave act.

"Why didn't you tell me?" Freddy couldn't handle losing Bella too.

She bit down on her lip as silent tears spilled down her cheeks. "Because I couldn't. You have no idea how much you being there for me helped me through some really dark times and I promise that, when I can, I'll be in contact."

"You shouldn't make promises like that," Andrei corrected her gruffly. "Hug or whatever y'all need to do, and then we need to go."

Freddy held his sister's shaking body close, trying not to think about when he would see her next. "I love you, Bella, and I swear you should have been the heir to Daddy's title."

"Oh, I always knew I would have done a better job of it than you," she said with a watery smile. "But you're stuck with it, and I swear, if you don't do a good job of living your life, I'll come back and nag you, no matter what my new name might be." She pulled him in close again. "Tell Harper goodbye for me and thank her for being a friend when I needed one the most."

Freddy felt her slip from his grasp, watching her go until she was lost from his sight. Closing his eyes against his grief, he steeled himself for what was to come next. If he lost Harper for good, he didn't know if he would ever be able to live with the pain that clawed at his heart.

HARPER CLOSED HER EYES, willing herself to let go of the feeling that flowed through her. She'd done it. Somehow, despite Freddy trying to sabotage her, she'd won. Harper Ferguson was the individual gold medal winner at the European Championships! Harper had never felt more miserable in her life.

"I can't believe it," Carol screamed in excitement. "I mean, I thought you could do it, but to actually do it." She began to rummage around in her pockets, pulling out pieces of straw and twine before finding a treat for Denny. "And the team came third." She blew out a deep breath. "I don't think my heart can handle it."

"I wouldn't celebrate too soon." Lionel sniffed. "Given the antics of your owner, I'll be quite amazed if the horse isn't disqualified. I, for one, certainly don't tolerate the team being brought into disrepute."

Harper stared at him, her mouth ajar. "What?" she finally managed.

A commotion sounded behind them, security grabbing hold of a frantically waving Freddy. "This is exactly the behavior I was talking about."

"What on earth is going on?" Carol whispered to Harper.

"I have no idea." Shedding his jacket, Freddy managed to give the beefy security men the slip, dodging their outstretched hands as he sprinted toward them. He was surprisingly fast. "Harper, I need to talk to you."

"Don't you think you've done enough damage with your antics today?" Lionel stepped between them. "I won't tolerate you anywhere near the team."

Freddy lowered his head in a bullish manner and kept his pace, the selector only moving at the last moment when it became abundantly clear that the charging man had no intention of stopping. "Lionel, old chap, you need to take it up with the FBI." He fished a business card out of his pocket.

"In fact, this is the number to call. Tell him Freddy told you to, and if you still have issues with me or Harper you can take it up with my barrister."

Harper felt like she'd fallen asleep watching a movie and had woken up to a different one. Fighting through the cobwebs of her disorientation, she could only gape at Freddy. Her heart clenched as he took her hand tenderly, gazing beseechingly into her eyes.

"I know you hate me, but please just listen to what I have to say and then, if you still feel that way, I'll go. I'll even sign over ownership of Denny to you. You guys belong together no matter what happens between us."

Tears burned her eyes as she nodded, floundering in a maelstrom of emotions. "I don't know what you could say that will make a difference."

"Dmitri was trying to blackmail me with Bella's safety to get you to do poorly because he bet against you. Then the FBI asked for my help, and now everything is fine. Or at least, I think it is."

Hysterical laughter bubbled up in Harper. It sounded so outlandish that it might just be true. You never could tell with Freddy.

"The FBI?" Carol asked dubiously.

Freddy gave her an unfriendly glare. "Go talk to Lionel over there. I'm sure he'll be able to give you the number to call."

The groom grinned at him. "I can't wait to get back home and tell this story at my local pub." Denny began to rub his head on her, leaving smears of black makeup. "It's time I put this fella away." She gave the two of them a sly wink. "I think you two have a lot to catch up on."

Harper didn't even notice them leave. Was it possible that it was true? Could she trust him? "I don't know what to say," she stammered fearfully.

The touch of his hand on her cheek was almost unbearable in its tenderness. "I know you don't trust me, and I understand why you reacted the way you did. Even I know the unreliable reputation I have, but I never really had a reason to be more, not till I met you." The hurt shadowing his self-mocking eyes stabbed at her. "But I love you, and I need to know if you still love me."

"You still love me after how I treated you?" Hope clawed its way through the other emotions raging inside her. She still didn't understand exactly what had happened, but she would eventually. What mattered now was that there was still a chance that she hadn't thrown everything away.

He gently traced the line of her jaw, her body tingling from the contact. "Haven't you realized I'm loyal to a fault? I love you, and there is nothing you can do to change that."

Love for him crashed into her in a great tidal wave. "I love you, too."

Freddy searched her eyes as if trying to prove to himself that she meant it. "I guess I need to work on becoming Mr Dependable."

"Why?"

"Because I have a horse and rider who I need to support in their dreams of getting to the Olympics."

"Well, Mr Dependable, you can start by giving me a kiss."

As his lips locked with hers, sealing forever his vow of love, Harper knew one thing—life with the man she loved was never going to be anything but exciting.

A tiny hand tugged at Freddy's pants leg as *God Save the Queen* played over the loudspeaker. Sighing, he reached down and picked up the miniature tyrant. "Ned, old chap, this moment isn't about you." He pointed out into the distance where a slender woman stood, proudly gazing at the English flag, gold medal around her neck as she grasped a bouquet of flowers tightly. Behind her, Denny stood proudly like he knew what he'd done, garland around his neck as Carol discreetly fed him treats. "Do you know how special it is to see someone achieve a dream?"

"Yeeya," Edward solemnly replied.

"I wish Bella could have been here," Chora said sadly. "Have you heard from her?"

"Not since you did. I think, after what happened, someone has laid down the law." Freddy liked to think that, wherever she was, his sister was watching Harper win her gold medal on TV, feeling like it was her moment too.

"I hope it was that cowboy she told you about," Cassie said, leaning past her new husband. "One day, when it's safe,

I can't wait to talk to her and find out what happened." Her eyes glowed at all the intel she could gather.

"Don't you dare," warned Stirling, her husband. "Leave Bella alone. I'm sure she's been through enough."

"But Stirling, imagine the movie you could make from it," she protested.

"I'd bloody watch it," Murphy agreed, rubbing her swollen belly.

"I know someone who could get us invites to the premiere," Alistair said to his pregnant wife.

"I didn't say I'd make it," Stirling said over Cassie's head.

"Didn't you say something in your vows about loving and obeying me?" Cassie asked tartly.

"That was a rookie mistake," Landon said, joining the fray.

Freddy listened to his friends' good-natured chatter. "Do you think they'll notice if I slip away?" he asked the little boy in his arms. Ned shook his head and held his arms out to his mother. Chora's focus remained firmly on the conversation on hand as, without thought, she gathered her toddler close.

Leaving the stands of the Olympic stadium, Freddy made his way to the warmup arena, waiting for Harper to complete her victory lap. Carol spied him and made her way over. "Are you ready?"

He grinned at her. "More than you could possibly imagine. You know what I need you to do?"

"Of course. Act natural, keep everyone away who might want to talk to her, take video."

He frowned at her. "I didn't ask you to video."

She grinned wickedly back at him. "Oh, that might just be something I decided to do. You can thank me later." Any retort from him was cut off as Harper and Denny appeared.

She still took his breath away. That mix of indomitable will and determination wrapped up in a gorgeous, intelligent package. For a man who could buy anything, it turned out that what he needed the most, money couldn't buy.

Freddy stepped forward and clasped her body to his, breathing in the mixture of horse, sweat and the delicate perfume that was all hers. "I'm so proud of you."

"I'm proud of me, too," she said giddily. "I don't think it's sunk in yet. It's like the perfect day I've dreamed about for so long and now it's too much."

"Do you think you would want to do it all again?" He wasn't sure if he was asking about the Olympics or something deeper.

"Oh my, yes." She breathed. "Every single thing."

"Well then, I guess I should jolly well plead my case." He took a step back and got down on bended knee, holding out a ring box. "Harper Ferguson, I love you, and being part of your dream has given me joy that I didn't know I would ever experience. Will you marry me?"

"I, ah—" Harper's hand flew to her mouth, Freddy's heart leapt to his throat. *Was she going to say no?* "Of course I'll marry you." Not even bothering to brush off the dirt from his immaculately tailored pants, he put the gold brilliant cut diamond ring on Harper's finger before she could change her mind. Just for good measure, he swept her into his arms and covered her face in kisses, leaving her giggling breathlessly.

"There was a rumor going around that the only way to keep coming to Olympics was to marry an athlete. I didn't want to take any chances," he said lightly, staring down at the woman who had just made him happier than he'd thought possible.

"Assuming I qualify for more, of course you would. You're an owner." Harper rolled her eyes at him, used to his need to hide his vulnerability behind jokes.

"This is more secure. At the next one, I'll be able to say 'that's my wife up there.'"

Wife. Funny how there was no longer a bachelor to be found amongst his friends. Life was amazing and richer than it had ever been when they'd been just bachelor billionaires. Running a thumb lazily over the sensitive part of the nape of Harper's neck, he smiled smugly when she shivered deliciously. *Yes, funny how it had turned out that each of them had found love from the dust.* Shaking away his frivolity, he returned to the serious matter at hand—kissing his fiancée.

THE END

As an Indie Author, reviews help me get my books noticed. If you enjoyed reading Freddy's and Harper's story as much as I did writing it, please leave a review. It will make all the difference to me.

If you loved, *Gold Dust and the Billionaire,* sign up for my newsletter here to get free bonus's and exclusive news. Now, turn the page to discover two new series *The Brothers of Creekside Ranch* and *The Christmas Star Collection*

SNEAK PEAK – LEVI (BOOK ONE OF THE BROTHERS OF CREEKSIDE RANCH SERIES)

"Here are your documents," the man Bella had known as Andrei—she still didn't know his real name—said before throwing them one at a time on the table in front of her. "Driver's license, birth certificate, social security number, passport."

Curiously, she picked them up. "Rebecca Callaghan." *Gosh she was tired.* "So, what does this Rebecca Callaghan do for a job?" She fingered the mousy brown wig they'd put her in. "Judging from how she looks, a dinner waitress?"

Andrei laughed. "It's good that you still have your sense of humor, especially after your long flight here. Tomorrow, you will have another short one and then you'll see where you're going to be staying."

Bella wanted to cry. When she'd first been approached by the FBI, it had seemed so noble. At least, that's what she'd told herself when she'd agreed to help them put Dmitri away. Deep in her soul, it had been to save herself. Each day, she'd felt that she was closer to him killing her in one of his games that he'd liked to play. Now the harsh reality was sinking in. She was far from home, looking like a drudge, and she didn't know when she'd be able to speak to her brother, let alone see him.

Biting her lip, she forced the tears away. Her parents hadn't raised her to have the famous British stiff upper lip for nothing. *I survived Dmitri, I can survive this.*

∽

"Levi, I appreciate your assistance in this matter." Andrew, his old Navy SEAL buddy, extended his hand out. "You understand the need for discretion?"

"Sure thing." He took a seat opposite him. "You were pretty vague on the phone." It had come as a surprise to hear from him, especially asking for help with planting a rose bush. "I trust the rose is here?"

"She is. I can't tell you anything, you understand." Andrew held his gaze.

"Copy. The less I know the better." Levi cracked his knuckles. "The timing works out well."

"I thought so." Andrew scratched at the back of his neck. "I guess it's time you meet her."

Curiously, he followed Andrew into the other room and stopped, eyeing the delicate beauty in front of him. The horrendous mousey brown wig did little to hide the delicate English rose complexion, nor the large albeit exhausted eyes, rimmed as they were in shadows of fatigue. Levi turned to his friend. "I don't think this is going to work. She's not cut out for where she's going."

"Excuse me?" the woman said in a posh British accent. "I think you'll find you'll quit before I do."

"Sweetheart, I'm a Navy SEAL. Quitting ain't in my vocabulary." He leaned closer to glower at her.

"I'm—" She stopped. Recovering, she glared down her

pert little nose at him. "Well, if I could tell you what I am, you'd be shaking in your boots before your betters."

"Good to see you two getting on."

"Who is this loathsome man?"

Andrew hid his smile when Levi glowered at him. "Rebecca, this is Levi. Levi, this is Rebecca. Rebecca, you are going to be the nanny to his little sister on their family ranch."

"Which means, sweetheart, I'm your boss."

"Like heck it does." Alarmed, she glanced toward Andrew in appeal. "Surely there are other, better, more suitable options."

"Unfortunately for you and me both, I'm it." Levi liked the way she bit down hard on her bottom lip as she thrust her stubborn little chin out. "So, Beccy, you better start liking the idea." Good Lord knew he was starting to.

Levi available on Amazon and in Kindle Unlimited here

Good Lord, she was tired. Veronica didn't know the last time she'd had more than a day off. Heck, she couldn't even remember when she'd had a single day off. She tried not to complain. She was living the dream of every actress who came to Tinseltown. But having come off eight back-to-back movies, the last one about sex trafficking had sapped the last of her creative energies.

"I have a message from Anton," her agent's assistant said as she sunk exhaustedly into the chair. "He asked me to give it to you when you came in to see Herb."

Herb waved for his assistant to continue. Clearing her throat, she glanced nervously around before reading from her note. "My dearest Veronica." Again, the assistant looked at her boss. "Maybe I could just give it to Veronica and she can read it herself in private."

"I'm her agent. She doesn't have anything private from me," barked Herb. "Now, get on with it."

Again, she cleared her throat. "What we have is special." Veronica smiled. Anton was a sweetheart and the perfect fiancé. Since they'd become a couple a year ago, they'd been quite the celebrity pairing. That is, when they were in the same country. When had they last been in the same country? She couldn't remember.

"Um, I adore you, but it isn't working out for me. I hope we can continue to love and have the upmost respect for each other."

Veronica's stomach churned. "I don't understand."

"He broke up with you, Veronica. Deal with it. We have movies to make." Herb began to rifle through the scripts on his desk. "Did you read the romcom I sent you?"

Veronica stared, uncomprehending. "Anton broke up with me? Six weeks before Christmas?"

Herb gave her a cynical look. "Who cares about Christmas anyway?"

"I do!" Veronica jumped to her feet. "I do, and you and Anton and everyone else can go take a giant leap!"

The Cowboy's Christmas Star available on Amazon and in Kindle Unlimited here

ACKNOWLEDGMENTS

A debt of gratitude to my editor Rebekah Groves for her patience with me.

Another big thanks to Megan from Designed with Grace for her cover design.

To my amazing beta readers and street team, you guys rock and I couldn't do it without you.

And finally to my fabulous alpha reader Trixie Norman, for all the late nights of reading and endless questions about your thoughts.

Red Dust and The Billionaire

Wild horses couldn't drag this couple to happily ever after…right?

Buy Now

Star Dust and The Billionaire

It'll take more than star dust and Hollywood magic to get *this* couple to happily ever after…

Buy Now

Gold Dust and The Billionaire

Freddy's Story Coming Soon…

Buy Now

The Brothers of Creekside Ranch Series

Levi

Levi and Bella's story

Pre Order Now

Amos

Pre Order Now

Elijah

Pre Order Now

Cowboy Christmas Series

The Mistletoe Collection

Boots and Mistletoe

Cowboy boots, mistletoe, and a holiday do-over…

Buy Now

The Cowboy Under the Mistletoe

It'll take more than the magic of the season to help this grump find her happily ever after...

Buy Now

Mistletoe and the Billionaire's Cowgirl

He's the last man she wants this holiday season. Too bad he's exactly what she needs...

Buy Now

The Christmas Star Collection

The Cowboy's Christmas Star

Pre Order Now

Her Reluctant Christmas Cowboy Star

Pre Order Now

Barrels and Hearts series

Available on Amazon and Kindle Unlimited

A Bull Rider's Paradise

The prequel to the Barrels and Hearts series. True love is only the beginning....of the story. Find out where it all began with Ana and Eduardo. Sometimes finding love is easy. It's keeping it that's hard.

Buy here

A Cowgirl's Dream

An Aussie cowgirl far from home. A handsome Brazilian bull rider. Can they have a rodeo love story of their dreams?

Buy Now

A Cowgirl's Heart

An Aussie cowgirl in need. Her childhood friend to the rescue. Can friendship turn into a love story?

Buy Now

A Cowgirl's Passion

One feisty cowgirl. One steadfast Brazilian bull rider. Will she see what is right in front of her?

Buy Now

A Cowgirl's Pride

An Aussie cowgirl from the wrong side of the tracks. A handsome equine vet. Can they find a way to have their happy ever after?

Buy Now

A Cowgirl's Love

A young Aussie cowgirl. A widowed rancher. Does age matter when it comes to love?

Buy Now

A Cowgirl's Movie Star

A fiery cowgirl with big dreams. A movie star far from home. When their two worlds collide, will their love be strong enough to hold them together or will they be pulled apart

Buy Now

A Cowgirl's Billionaire

A cowgirl adrift. A broken billionaire cowboy. Can he free himself from the past to be the man she needs now?

Buy Now

ABOUT THE AUTHOR

Edith MacKenzie or Eddie Mac to her friends is an author of sweet and wholesome contemporary cowboy romance. They say in literary circles to write what you know, and Eddie has certainly taken that to heart. Before embarking on a writing career, she trained horses professionally and brings that wealth of knowledge to her writing.

Now a mum to a boy and girl, as well as wife, she delights with her tales of strong cowgirls and their adventures in finding love. When not weaving the love stories of her characters, she enjoys hanging out with her family and animals, as well as reading, fishing and camping.

Just remember—once a cowgirl, always a cowgirl.

facebook.com/EddieMacAuthor
instagram.com/edith_mackenzie_author
amazon.com/Edith-MacKenzie
bookbub.com/profile/edith-mackenzie
twitter.com/edith_mackenzie

www.ingramcontent.com/pod-product-compliance
Lightning Source LLC
Chambersburg PA
CBHW030434120726
47903CB00003B/954